Collecting Dust

FRESH VOICES IN SHORT FICTION AND POETRY

—

EDITED BY

HUDSON WARM

Collecting Dust

Cover design: Damonza
Formatting: Enchanted Ink Publishing

ISBN: 978-1-7354098-2-5

Library of Congress Control Number: 2022910707

Printed in the United States of America

Collecting Dust

Contents

Laundry

Sophie Miller, New York
TW: Sexual Assault

When you can't move, your thoughts move much quicker
Crazed
Panicked
Frantic
But then they slow down like the last
Spoonful in those glass ketchup bottles
And you wonder if they'll ever fall

Your mind becomes a far-off voice
Separated
Alarms are still flashing
But it's as if someone drew the curtains
Covered the satellite
And everything goes to static

When you see your shirt on the ground
You remember how it feels to be

Silenced by the fear
The unrelenting fear
The wrongness
And more than anything, the dirt that has wedged itself
within the fibers of the shirt
From being on the ground for far too long
The dirt that will not let up
Never goes away
Always follows
Silent but unimaginably strong

And when you feel the phantom hands
Scraping down your back
Leaving paths of grime behind—
Balling up the hem of your shirt in fists that rip the soul
From your body
As the shirt is pulled over your head
And you want to say stop
But all you can manage is a desperate grab for the shirt as
it falls to the ground
You wrinkle
Contract
Become as small as possible
Because crumpling is the only way to hide
From those hands that are not there

The world goes still
You take a shaky breath and look over at your shirt
But you cannot pick it up
So it just stays there
In the corner
Collecting dust

MORNING.

MORNING.

Rays of Old

Danielle N. Bartholet, Houston, TX

The sunlight bathes over me.
It renews me, revitalizes my
wounded soul from the night's darkness.
The sun knows me like an old friend, witnessing my joys
and sorrows from afar,
comforting in its everlasting presence high in the sky for
my eyes to look towards
when I am lost and alone.

It has seen my tears, my smiles, my ugliness, and my
beauty. And still each morning it returns for more of me.
To learn my pieces through the sunrises,
through the oranges and pinks, the reds and yellows.
The sun has seen what hurts, has felt my soul's longing as
acutely as its own.
Those are the scars that stay, from which hurt remains
only an ache.

But it also sees wounds, open and bleeding, that exist
only to become another one of those scars, reminding me.

As each ray dances over the morning dew gathering on
the grass like the purest liquid gold, as I shed the skin of
yesterday to greet possibility with open arms and a soft
kiss on each of its solar-dusted cheeks.

The sun casts its glow, and I am freed.

Soft Beginnings

Kimberly Swartz, Washington

There was something about waking up in the morning that sat well with me. It could be the sunrays shining through the window, the soft warm bedding, or the last wisps of dreams slipping away for another night.

It could be waking up next to him. Alex, I could almost always catch him still asleep, and it was pretty. He was one of those pretty sleepers. The ones whose lips were in a half pout and whose nose wrinkled as they dream. He would always have a hand halfway extended to me, as if he wanted to reach out but knew better. He always knew to ask and I loved him for it.

His golden hair was splayed out on the pillow, fanning around him in a halo in the sun. Alex looked like an angel, something to rival gods. His golden skin, healthy and, as always, well taken care of, blazed with a slight flush.

I pushed myself up to an elbow so I could get a closer look. The blanket, a heavy white polka dot monster that went with nothing in our room, was low on his bare chest.

I reached out with my hand and slowly ran my finger through the soft chest hair. Another thing to love about him, he always took time to take care of each part of his body—whether his face or toes.

He huffed and batted my hand away like he was shooing a bug. I pulled back and watched as he slowly woke up. It started with his face scrunching before relaxing. He turned his face toward the pillow and slowly rolled his shoulders. He yawned and arched his back off the bed, the blanket falling off him more. I could see the soft V line in his stomach. Slowly, his eyes fluttered open, and he smiled.

"Morning," he said.

I could wake up this way every morning and I would be a happy man.

A Romance Bottled in Memory

Alexandra Elwell, New York

It is more of a collective than a singular memory, my romance, and to tell it, I have to relay to you some regales from a few years of my youth. Though I can remember little, I can assure you that the romance Antoine and I had was something so idyllic and picturesque it seemed to have fallen out of a fable and onto our laps. He was in the same year as me at Metropolitan Montessori School and I spied him looking at me from across the tables in Room C. I quickly averted my eyes when I noticed his gaze and returned to teaching a friend how to braid with no prior knowledge of what a braid even was; I was eccentric like that. We became fast friends, at one point creating a blockade furnished in pillows and play chairs in my room with our backs pressed against the door, hindering the adults from getting in. We spewed insults at them of the highest sophistication touching on nudity and potty time as we giggled and mercilessly destroyed them with our artillery of refined barbs. We finally let them into my room after we'd won the battle. They were too unaware to have known they were even waging a war; our toddler intelligence was too extreme for them to contend with. I have very little memory of Antoine, but I know that our romance superseded that of Jack and Rose, though we, too, had an iceberg of our own to drag us apart. He moved. Possibly back to France he went, and with him my young heart. I remember seeing him off and trudging to his house in the rain, the wind bending our umbrellas backward and causing little me to stumble. But I was relentless and persevered through the thunderous gale and treacherous winds. I was Odysseus, and the tempest we had fought for hundreds of blocks was worse than the one inflicted by Poseidon. But I won. No, I did not land shipwrecked on the shores of Scheria, and no, I did not need the guidance of Athena to help me emerge unscathed. It was my pure toddler love for Antoine that helped me battle the raging winds. With my hair sopping wet and clothes tattered, we arrived after our long expedition at his apartment. It was a blur, our final playdate, but I kept something of his after we had parted. I liked his fluffy doll, so I stole it, knowing I never would see him again and he probably would have lost it anyhow. For years, I kept it in my bucket of toys, turning to it when the others bored me. I got on with my hectic preschool life as he voyaged down the street to another school. Who would tend to the masses at Metropolitan if not me? I knew that he must have pined for his lost love from Texas and must have been broken with anguish at losing someone as incredible as me. That wonderful period of time I spent with Antoine, that I can recall, is something my future husband will have to work hard to surmount. After all, romance is yelling potty words, walking in mild rain, and stealing fluffy toys, is it not?

I returned to my duties with a heavy head. I led my group of friends—with matching sneakers and with our sacred bottle cap with a mirror glued inside—on our adventures. I moved on from Antoine after a few hours of mourning and decided it best to search for a man who didn't now live in Australia. I must have blocked my flings from my memory as a lot of pre-K and kindergarten is a blur, though I don't know why. I do know, however, that it was my incredible genius that discovered the bush of poisonous berries in a pot on the roof. It was the hallowed bottle cap that led me to the red berries dangling off the small branches. I knew without even needing to consult our resident scientist, my best friend at the time, Grace, that these berries were indeed harmful. Yet again, the adults were incompetent, and I asked my fellow tykes, "How could these so-called 'teachers' not spy the toxic berries with their deleterious effects in the corner of our garden?" We sent messengers, equipped with their state-of-the-art G-Force sneakers, to notify the rest of the class to steer clear of the beady red sirens. Us toddlers were the fishermen with our wriggling hunger analogous to their lust for the beautiful creatures on the rocky coastlines to wreck their ships. I could not let my fellow youths succumb to the unknown fate that the tempting berries could have, so we screamed and shouted, very unlike our normal playing. After ten whole minutes, the danger was gone. We spent so much time worrying about the berry bush that we became hungry, so we asked for snacktime. Our phenomenal attention spans were broken for the very first time in our lives by food. Thankfully, the crisis was averted as we forgot the bush existed and continued to play until someone got a bloody nose. But not Antoine; he was gone. My one true love living in Amsterdam, or on Amsterdam Avenue—same thing. I forgot about him after a long period of time—the time it took me to eat dinner—and moved on as I tried to locate any sweet treats in my house. I decided after we parted that I was a savior to all who could not be tied down by anyone—definitely not by Antoine.

Road to Ronda

Alex Cheng, Connecticut

The last time I visited Ronda, I borrowed laughter. Worries disintegrated, what-ifs dried up under a Spanish sun. Back then, I'd ridden on a Los Amarillos tour bus that was bedecked with gold and green decals, but today, the company's name was a strange word I could not comprehend. The bus had many of the same elements, however: carnival-blue seats splattered with dippin-dot hues, phone chargers like open mouths mounted above, and air conditioning that gasped and wheezed and never seemed to catch its breath.

I entered the bus and settled on a seat one row from the back—it was the seat that I had used twenty-one years ago, Mom and Dad across the aisle, Lilly on my left. Now, I was alone. The silence gnawed at my ears like hoarfrost.

Putting my bag down beside me, I gazed at the line of buses parked helter-skelter outside my window, attempting to decipher a hidden message in their parking patterns that was not there. The scene felt like a doppelgänger of the Sevilla bus station from my youth. But even déjà vu can be manufactured when I'm desperate enough.

Behind the station, barely contained in the window's wingspan, cherry trees the color of half-digested cotton candy hid in plain sight. Most of them were still pink, although barely. Stray flowers fluttered over the station floor, sticking onto car wheels, hoping to hitch a ride out of Sevilla. When I pried my eyes away from the window, I saw a short balding man sitting across from me in the very seats Mom and Dad had once chosen.

Out of all the rows available, the bald man had decided to infringe on mine; annoyance bubbled inside of me. I bit my lip, massaged the tension from my hands, and plugged in a well-worn playlist.

Bzz. Bzz. The lyrics were interrupted by my ringtone.

Chelsea.

I had briefly skimmed over her fifty-four messages and twenty-two voicemails before I had boarded. Her voice was desert-cracked, a medley of longing and alarm. *I'll be back soon.* I had wanted to text her, but the words dried on my fingertips, then withered and died. Before I resumed the music, my eyes flitted over my phone background, a monochrome image of our wedding day. Her dress was long, white, ethereal. My suit was night terror-blue.

The music consumed my guilt.

Soon, the bus hissed and began to crawl slowly from the station onto the main road. Shards of sunlight spilled across the seats. Motes of dust became illuminated against waves of lights and shadows. The bus lurked past foreignly familiar structures: a plaza from an old photo, the exterior of a rustic alcazar. Small streets broadened, and large roads became narrow, winding paths that carved through the mountainous landscape of Andalucia.

"Could I borrow your phone charger?" The words of the balding man startled me.

"No, sorry," I promptly replied, shifting my bag closer up against my hip. "I'm going to need it soon."

"Please." The man reached toward his back pocket and fumbled his thick ungainly fingers across the hemming of his wallet. "Take fifteen euros." He fanned the lime-green bills. "I need to document my journey to Ronda for my daughter back home." He slurred his Rs and occasionally fumbled the pronunciation of a word or two and had to restart. "I told her I would give her the photos—please."

I examined the man again before reconsidering his request; his eyes were green and large, and his forehead was wrinkled, yet somehow forgiving. He seemed to be the type of man who would ride buses alone and then tell his one or two friends that even he, a balding middle-aged baker, could still be enthralled by adventure.

"Sure." The old man's kind features won me over. I was in no rush to reply to Chelsea anyway. I groped around the outer pocket of my bookbag, hand clasping around an orphaned white cord.

"Thanks," he mumbled, a gentle smile spreading across his face and his hands again reaching for the bills.

"No need," I said, motioning the money away. The man shrugged.

For a while, there seemed to be no time at all: hills, cliffs, valleys, hills, the backyard of Andalucia perpetually looped. Big-bellied cattle lazed; snaking rivers sauntered so slowly that they might have been still. Soon, the silence was cleaved by the murmurs of the bald man, with laughs and long pauses dispersed in between. *Familia. Padre. Final.* I recognized a few of the cognates from my brief stints in Spanish class.

The bald man continued to talk with a lightness that bettered his posture. He was a father, I pieced together, probably talking to his daughter that he had mentioned earlier. I wondered where he was from: Mexico, Uruguay, or even Spain. Maybe he was from the country's northeast corner and lived on a small farm in rural Galicia. His daughter had never left the indoors because of a rare allergy to the sun, yet had always wanted to see the rest of Spain. She had long brown hair that would look magnificent sun-bleached, and crystalline-blue eyes that were so pale they may have turned to water if she stepped outdoors. So the old man spent the rest of his life savings to travel and send home personalized videos of the world his daughter could never step into, his vitality surging every time he serenaded her dancing eyes, as any good father should. I repeated those last words in my head: *as any good father should.* When I glanced over at the man's wrinkled neck, shoulders shuddering from the shadow of a laugh, the story almost seemed true.

A dozen additional songs had passed by the time the balding man handed me back my charger. The songs left a different warmness around my chest that the peeking sun could not have; it was warmth tinged with familial lyrics. With every passing word, I heard Dad's voice booming in the background, however faint. I knew that he would fill in the words that I missed. Before the thought could wither away, I pulled up my Notes app. *Fill in her words,* I typed out below a list consisting of *Travel somewhere beautiful (Ronda?)* in all caps and *Play Dice.*

The old man turned suddenly and handed the cable back by the head like an exotic snake. "Thank you."

"No problem," I replied, avoiding his eyes.

"You're American, right?" he asked before I could plug my music back in.

I turned around curiously, juggling my right earbud in my hands like a die; Dad and I had shot dice on our last trip to Ronda, Mom's lap, our table, our daily quota of ice cream, the wagers. "Yes, why?"

"If you don't mind, could you tell me what it's like there?"

"What it's like?" I fleetingly thought of Chelsea and our small loft. Then to my childhood home, where warmth leaked from cracks in the brick. Then, momentarily, to the town orphanage. I grimaced. "Well, I don't really know. I haven't been to many places besides my hometown."

"Do you live near Missouri?"

For a second, I was amazed. Shocked more so. "Yeah, Kansas City. How did you know?"

The man expelled a shallow cough-like laugh. "A lucky guess. Oh, I've heard things."

"What have you heard?" I shifted upright and sheathed my earbuds into their charging case. Then, guilt enveloped me like a wet blanket. Missouri. Home. Chelsea. But Ronda is magical, I assured myself. When I go back, I'll be ready.

"My daughter reads a lot of Mark Twain. *Huckleberry Finn*'s her favorite. Do you happen to live near Jackson's Island?"

I shook my head no.

"It is an island in the book, and she insists that it's a real place as well." The man let out another laugh, although this one was from deeper in his body, a lung or heart, but not yet the full stomach-gulping guffaw Dad used to say was good for the soul. "She wants to move there one day, to traverse the same land that her heroes did." By now, any dregs of his former laughter had been swallowed by a receding tide of melancholia. "She said that they were beckoning her to come over. That now, she could finally make the trip without any monetary constraints—"

"*Llegaremos en treinta minutos*," the voice of the driver interrupted; there were so few people, the loudspeaker was not necessary.

"*Bien, gracias*," the man called back, albeit weakly. He was not a fragile man, I could tell, but something inside of him had fractured.

I shifted closer up on my seat, intrigued by my companion. He talked about his daughter like any great father would. Like any great father *should*. "Great, when is she coming over?" I queried. "If she needs, I can help her move in or introduce her to my wife and—" But I stopped myself before more words seeped out.

He seemed to wilt even more. "I appreciate the offer, but, you see, Jackson's Island is an uninhabitable place."

"What do you mean?"

"It's—" There was a snuffle in his voice, like a chip in a once-ornate teacup. "It's in the middle of a river. Accessible only by boat and with no other inhabitants. It was always a dream, and it will always be just that, you see. She never even got the chance to live it out."

"Never got the chance? But I—"

"She's in hospital now." His words arrived in a slur as if they had been carbonating since the moment our conversation began. "She has always been sickly, but this time, the doctors fear that it's something worse."

"Oh?" The image of a sun-allergic daughter capsized into the whitewater of the Mississippi. His daughter, gone. Then how could he be a good father?

"Have you been to Ronda before?" the man asked, changing course suddenly.

"Once before. A long, long time ago." I wondered if he considered twenty-one years a long time ago. Physically, maybe not, but emotionally, mentally, we were all different people back then.

"Do you still remember?"

"How could I not? The bridge, the gates, the hike, it is the most beautiful place I have ever seen."

He nodded, but never looked up. "It really is."

"What is your favorite part?"

After a pregnant pause, he began. "The gorge under the Casa del Rey Moro is a close second. I've taken my daughter there many times. Her *abuelo* used to live across the street. We'd get gelato, then make the walk down, her *abuelo's* knees nearly giving out." I knew that the smile he gave was not procured in the moment—it had been produced many years ago, and only now did he choose to unveil it. He continued. "The city's beautiful and all, but for me, it was always the people. I wouldn't have gone to Ronda every week to see my father if it hadn't been for her." He chuckled. "It was the atmosphere I think I loved. The people, our connection, more than any single landmark."

I took my phone out, crossing out *Travel somewhere beautiful (Ronda?). Connections > travel?* I scribbled next to the strikethrough, although it didn't seem right. Dad had brought us to see the most beautiful place in the world.

Under the looming bridge, he had healed a ruptured relationship with Mom. It had all been in front of the most magnificent background; there was something in Ronda, something that I needed to uncover.

I stabbed the undo arrow until the original text returned.

"What about you? Why did you decide to come back?"

I shrugged. "For the memories, I guess."

"Alone?"

I nodded. "Shouldn't you be with your daughter?" I asked impulsively. *As any good father should* danced on my tongue, a phantom.

The old man brought his hands to his veined temples, but otherwise, seemed comfortable with the question. "She wants to see Ronda for the last time. I will video call her as I walk through the city. It'll be different, but it'll be something. I was supposed to fly to Missouri, but the doctors don't know if there will be enough time." He sighed again, but he didn't shrink with his exhales; in a way, he grew. "Is that your wife?" He pointed to my phone's lock screen.

"Yeah." My voice trailed off like a disfigured wisp of secondhand smoke.

"Why haven't you come with her?" It was his turn to be nosy.

"I needed some, uh, alone time." My eyes fell silent while his gaze hovered over my hair like a loose-fitting shawl.

"An argument?"

"She's. Expecting."

"If you ask me, just run away and stay in Spain." The man laughed. This time, however, the laugh vibrated his shoulders and squeezed his eyes closed—it was a stomach laugh. He turned serious. "But, why come to Ronda, then?"

"I-I." My words stumbled, pushed against my ribs, but refused to pass the barrier of my teeth. "I need help." I finally blurted out.

"With what?" His words were curt like the slap of a wave.

I shrunk. "With being a father."

The big man unleashed a laugh that filled the bus like a hymn sung by a chain-smoker, momentarily vanquishing the shadow in his eyes. Nearly. "Why ask me? Go ask your own father!" He continued to laugh until his sorrow returned. "I was never the best father to her anyway. Now here I am, an old man running to Ronda, unsure whether it is love or guilt that drives me there. Perhaps, my friend, it is a mix of both. You should call your father when you have the time."

"My dad, mom, and sister died when I was eight."

He waited for me to say more.

"And, Ronda, well. We laughed over dinner, stayed up late playing dice, took hikes up and down the gorge. We learned the language together. There is magic here I can't quite grasp elsewhere. At home, we argued. Punches, cusses; once, shattered glass. But, there, all was well. For once."

"I can't be the father that I saw growing up." I continued, my voice looking for a rung to clasp onto. "I have to remember what it was, how Dad made it all weave together so for two weeks we sang out the word *familia*. It doesn't make any sense back in Kansas City. None of it. I'm just going to let Chelsea down."

For a while, I scrolled on my phone. Up my list. Then when the page relented, down again. There were only two bullet points so far, phrases I had lingered over since the pregnancy was announced. Maybe in Ronda, I could uncover more.

"I should've taken her to Missouri and Jackson's Island all those weekends instead of Ronda," the old man eventually replied bluntly. By now, the five minutes until arrival notice had been announced. In the distance, Ronda's historical center emerged over a tree line, the city's individual buildings like faraway gravestones in a cemetery of thought.

"Trust me, Ronda's better," I said.

But the old man just shook his head, his hands finding refuge in worn pockets. "It's not about what's better or prettier." His voice sounded removed, as if now when his mouth shifted, his words came from elsewhere.

I glanced down at my notes one last time, then

looked back up at my muse, the city. "The beauty here heals relationships as it did for my parents. You don't understand—"

"No!" His voice flared, a passion that had lain dormant until now sparking to life. His eyes, as if unpenned, looked for someplace to stabilize. "It doesn't matter where you are or how far away you are from Ronda or whether you are at home or on vacation. It's—it's—it's." He took a deep breath in a failed attempt to compose himself. "You can't just take notes and be a good father. You've got it all wrong."

A sudden frustration flared around my ribs, and its grip momentarily left me without breath. "Then help me! You're a father, a son. You know what it takes." The bus slowed as the roads transitioned from paved to cobblestone, the wheels hitching like a nagging cough over every bump we passed.

"When I was your age, I had all the same questions," he said, his tone barely a whisper. His stubby fingers with low-cut nails scratched around his hairy arms, but they left no white trails. "Being a father is hard. But it can't come from me to tell you how to be a dad. It can't come from your dad either, or an uncle, or the Internet. When you're Ronda-less, Missouri-less, think about what you want to be as a father, a mentor, a friend. No list can help you with that."

The shadows of the Ronda bus station quickly silenced the engine. Then, the old man, backpack slung over his shoulder, phone dialing a soon-to-be discontinued number, got up and didn't look back as he exited the bus. As any great father should.

Leaving Words on the Street

Sowon Kim, South Korea

writing stories
is leaving shoes
on the street,
hoping someone will
find them,
hold them close,
listen and understand.
        for the greatest writers
        are born
        with the desire
        to spread a message
        through the words
        they type.
                and all the grief,
                the sadness,
                the pain,
                that is as heavy

as a neutron star,
can be released
from the cage of one's heart,
just by knowing that
their work could help
someone find peace
in the midst of mayhem.

TWILIGHT.

TWILIGHT.

Tea for Nobody

María F. Bergero, Argentina

Matilda was solving a crossword on her velvet couch, like every Sunday afternoon, when the knocking on the door startled her. She spied the visitor through the peephole, and her heart sped up. It was Thomas Peters, the neighbor with honest eyes and a contagious smile. The one person who made her feel like a teenager with a secret crush.

Their interactions consisted of flirty and awkward small talk, but gossip kept Matilda well-informed about his marital status. He was divorced, just like her. Thomas stood outside with both hands inside his pockets, with statuesque elegance.

"Hi, Thomas! What a surprise," Matilda said, fidgeting with her hair.

"Matilda! I hope I'm not interrupting you."

"Not at all." Her mind went blank at the sight of his smiling eyes. They both nodded at each other without saying a word, and then Matilda's brain came back to life. "Oh, can I do something for you?"

"I'm hanging some paintings and I can't find my hammer," he said, rubbing the back of his neck. "Could you lend me yours? I mean, if you have one, of course."

Although Matilda wasn't a clumsy person, she dropped screws and pliers from the toolbox in the rush to get the hammer. She floated back to Thomas and gave it to him.

"My savior! Thank you. I'll bring it back in ten minutes. Won't be long." Thomas's silky voice filled the air with sparks.

Now and then, Matilda had the courage to leave her comfort zone, but it happened when she least expected it—an inner storm breaking out of nowhere.

"Would you like to stay for tea when you come back?" she blurted, holding her breath and swallowing the embarrassment.

"For sure! Sounds great!" He smiled.

She regretted her impulsiveness, her wildness. Dating was unthinkable for Matilda at the moment, since she considered herself too old for it. She had forgotten how to relax and how to talk to men. But there she was, next to the door with both hands on her face, thinking that the only way to make the evening work was by preparing what she had offered: tea.

The tea cabinet, painted green with sunflowers, waited to be opened. Matilda prepared her teas with caution; they were powerful. Whatever she pictured while brewing, the guest would see as a vivid memory after one sip. Her stomach ached with wicked butterflies. She had never used her gift for romantic purposes before.

When Matilda's father passed away, she gave a cup of tea to her mother, Anna, so it would soothe the pain. Anna sobbed for days; she'd felt guilty for having had an argument with her husband on the same day he'd died. Matilda feared for her mother's health, so she brewed lavender tea and pictured her father's last day as a joyful one. Anna drank the tea, and golden tears had rolled down her face. Her last tears of grief. Matilda was a proud daughter.

Other times, she wasn't as proud of her magic... Like the time she made tea for her boss—a grumpy man who didn't recognize her achievements and kept treating her as his assistant (she wasn't). The smell of chamomile and lemongrass had allured him to drink. Two seconds later, purple smoke had emerged from his mouth. He gave Matilda a promotion.

Although fear bubbled within her every time she made tea, her gift had only brought positivity to dark situations, she thought.

She opened the tea cabinet: a world of choices. First, she picked the herbs and the tea to be blended. Inside the cabinet, there were thirty tins filled with dried leaves and ingredients. The smallest details in the brewing had a direct influence on the memory. She closed her eyes, took a deep breath, and began.

Their story had actually begun back in the days when they only were neighbors who occasionally flirted. A freshly divorced Matilda had gone to the beach with her friends for the holidays.

On a humid night, they went to a bar and had tequilas. She danced to the rhythm of salsa, dressed in red, with her wavy locks touching her waist.

"Hey, you got that guy hypnotized over there," Matilda's friend told her.

Thomas was having a drink when his eyes met hers in a spicy complicity. His hair looked disheveled and his face youthful. They didn't say a word to each other, at least verbally, because their eyes were indeed talking. He moved closer and asked her to dance. That they were neighbors didn't make it awkward; it was as if they had always wanted to dance together. Thomas then stopped to take a bunch of jasmines from a centerpiece on a table. He tucked the flowers behind her ear.

Matilda put jasmine pearls, a stick of cinnamon, and green tea leaves into the infuser. It was its enchanting scent that would bring up that piece of memory: Matilda's hair smelling of jasmines, their love blossoming. But there had to be conflict in the story, or it wouldn't be credible.

After dancing, they walked under the starry night.

"I'm so glad I ran into you tonight. I'd like to spend more time with you," he said.

"I enjoy your company. A lot."

He leaned in for a kiss, but she stopped him.

"I'm sorry. I want this to work, but I'm not ready yet," she said and ran away, hair in the wind, hand on her chest.

A few seconds before the water boiled, Matilda poured it in the teapot, soaking the herbs and leaves from the infuser. Now she had to wait; the steeping took four dreadful minutes.

Years passed and they kept in touch, but merely as friends. The night at the beach was now a bygone memory, but one so warm that it lulled them to sleep on the roughest nights.

The steeping time was over, and Matilda held the teapot close to her lips. "Soul mates," she whispered.

On a stormy night, Thomas showed up at her door, soaking wet. "I can't get you out of my mind, Matilda." The night wrapped up in a passion stronger than the thunderstorm. A night he would remember as spicy as the cinnamon notes from the tea.

A few weeks later, the romance had flourished. She woke up every day to the smell of hot pancakes to find him cooking and singing in the kitchen. His touch was a burning candle on her skin every single time. They were a blend made in heaven. He saw how divine she was but respected her humanity, her freedom.

They spent the evenings having tea, solving crosswords together, reading books, talking about existential matters, or just walking in the park. And the sparks, the fire, the awkward giggles from the beginning remained present.

Tea was ready.

The round table in her garden looked perfect under the pale blue sky, next to an ivy wall, and over the fresh-cut grass. Matilda placed a mint tablecloth over it and arranged the teacups over their matching pink saucers. She placed down a jar of honey, the intimidating teapot filled with magic, and a humble centerpiece with jasmines.

A knock on the door startled her, and Matilda danced her way to answer. He was back. Tool in hand, hair fixed, and wearing a different T-shirt.

"I feel lucky. A hammer and an invitation on the same day."

"It's a thank you for returning the hammer," Matilda said, acting laid-back. "Not that I thought you'd steal it. You know what I mean." She felt her cheeks turn strawberry red, so she hurried to the small table, guiding her guest.

"I hope you like jasmine green tea." The nature, the flowers, and Matilda's subtle herbal fragrance would allure anyone.

Thomas sat and fidgeted while Matilda poured the tea in his cup.

"Um, Matilda, I appreciate you inviting me for tea, but I have to tell—"

"Oh, I get it. You don't have to stay. I don't want you to feel obligated."

"No, it's not that at all. It's just that I hate tea."

Silence filled the garden, poisoning the air. Even the birds shut up in horror. The worst possible outcome of the evening was now happening.

"I'm a coffee type of person." He smiled the words away.

If there was a moment to call things off, it was now. She preferred to keep it platonic and call it a day. Dream of what could have been.

"Oh, I'm sorry. I didn't know." Matilda's eyes widened.

"No worries. You didn't have to know."

"Maybe we can do this another time." She took a step back.

"I—I don't mind. I'd enjoy the evening by talking to you without a drink, anyway." He shrugged. His eyes studied Matilda's face, as if there he'd find answers.

Matilda froze and mumbled that she had run out of coffee, but the words felt weak in her mouth. A fear of talking gripped her, as if only by pronouncing a word, Thomas would discover her secret.

She sat down opposite him with the face of a traumatized person. She thought of all the possibilities. What if he stayed and they had coffee? What would she say? What if she said something wrong? What if she didn't even like him after all?

"I'm being annoying, right?" he said with worry in his voice.

Matilda shook her head, focused on the thin lines around his eyes, took a deep breath, and surrendered to whatever awaited.

"You know, I must have coffee somewhere."

"Great! I'll help you look for it." He grinned.

Change

Lauren Redwood, Canada

The joyous time of year circles around,
but this present is an odd-shaped moment.
We fill our days with laughter not to drown,
knowing it is the only component.

Every leaf falls stiffly upon the snow,
almost as if it can feel the unease.
But through new seasons of life, we all grow,
so, when tough moments come, it'll be a breeze.

We always expect the cold, not the bite.
As our boots crunch the snowflakes scatter.
Minds wander to places wonted for night,
the places we conceal and hide away.

The peculiar part is not seasons,

nor is it the biting and dreadful cold,

but how our association deepens,

expressive thoughts from the young to the old.

The Mysterious Knocker

Alexandria Johnson, Malaysia

Three knocks I heard at the door.

Too lazy to open my eyes or check the time on my mobile, I let the knocks die out like a day-old candle. Soon, the knocking tempo began to slow down. *Knock.... Knock.... Knock.... Knock... Knock... Knock.*

Then, the knocks suddenly became louder, as if the knocker had been storing energy in his knuckles. Whoever he was, he was knocking furiously on my door, making me explode in anger. Veins of vexation started bulging through my skin; even though they were invisible in the dark, I could feel the rage rising in me. It was the middle of the night. *Who the hell could be knocking at this hour?*

Who might it be? In the dead of night? A mass murderer? A ghost? A thief? *Okay, why am I thinking the scariest things? Now I can't sleep.* My overthinking brain didn't shut off either. Thank you very much, Mysterious Knocker, for striking this fear in me. I kicked my legs in the air and let out a frustrated groan while forcing my eyes closed. The noise was killing my manly beauty sleep and about to kill *me*. Even if it was a thief... *Ignore. Ignore. Ig...noreeeee!*

I drifted off again as the noise died out. As I slowly headed back to dreamland, another knock—this time, four knocks—echoed in the still night. My eyelids unwrapped themselves, and I let out a groan. Squinting through the blurriness, I glared at the door—opposite my wooden bed.

Grabbing my pillow, I pressed it hard against my ears, hoping to suffocate the noise, but instead, fear hammered in my chest. What if it was really a thief who wanted my blood? I scrambled out of bed and used the little energy from my body to push a heavy sofa against the door. *That should do.* No matter what size that entity might be, the important thing was my safety, and beauty sleep.

I squinted through the dark, thinking about what it could be that the intruder wanted. *No*, pretty sure there was nothing in this room they wanted.... except... maybe, *me dead.* Perhaps. But I was too tired to crack my head over this, so I went back to sleep.

Once I hit the pillow, crazy thoughts—did I padlock the front gate, did I lock the bedroom door—drowned my brain in madness. *But did I?* I rolled off the bed and dashed to the door. The doorknob turned ominously as I reached for it. Somebody was trying to break in. My heart dropped. *I am doomed.* But the door didn't open, meaning the door was locked! I clutched my racing heart. The intruder would go away soon, I told myself and went back to bed. I counted sheep, comforting myself. *Take anything, but please don't hurt me.* But the bogeyman kept putting nasty thoughts in my head.

My eyes were as wide open as an owl's when, *BANG*, a loud noise vibrated at the door. It sounded like a rifle had gone off. *Whoever you are, I don't even care anymore. Please, please, no more knocking. Just leave me be.*

A relieved smile crept onto my lips when the rattling knocks stopped. *Finally*, Mysterious Knocker had ended his annoying schemes. And I was able to go back to sleep without any disturbance. *Thank God.*

Morning came. Baby sparrows sang, more like screeched, at my window as they forced me out of bed. What a weird dream I'd had. I climbed over the sofa, opened the door, and headed outside to breathe in the fresh air. The sun shone directly in my eyes, as if showing me how powerful it looked. I grunted. *What a show-off!*

Footsteps grazed across the tiled floor behind me. I turned to see my wife switching on the water hose. "Wow, you are up early. Usually, you sleep in," I said. Her bluish-blond streaks of hair flew in the breeze as she aimed the water hose at me.

"What is wrong with you?" I threw my arms to block the splash, but the water spray was so strong that it drenched my side. I shouted at her to stop, but my words were futile, and my throat became sore.

"What is wrong with me? What's wrong with *you*?" she yelled.

"Huh?"

She kept spraying me and threw a watering can at me, which missed. Then she came closer, making the impact of the water beam stronger. Her eyebrows furrowed as she shouted, "How dare you! You sleepwalked and locked me out!"

I could have sworn I heard thunder echo in the distance. But I didn't recall sleepwalking—just had a very odd dream. I dreamt that I was locking every door in the house and barricading the bedroom, making sure to keep the demon out. She gave me a tight slap on the face, and my cheek turned crimson. "Didn't you hear me? I was knocking like crazy!"

Mental Pompeii

Maja Zajaczkowska, Poland

They saw what seemed to be tongues
of fire that separated and came to rest
on each of them (Acts 2:3).

We stood there, side by side, staring at the ardent flames rising up to the night sky. I felt his gaze on me, and with a blink of an eye, an insatiable fury began boiling in my veins.

"Is everything all right?" he asked, as if we had not just committed one of the most ridiculous crimes possible. If we were caught, we would most likely spend the rest of our lives behind bars, without the chance of parole.

"Certainly," I mumbled and felt his arms around me. We were the worst couple imaginable: a match made in hell. One may be pondering how we ended up in these ruins, surrounded by flames and dirt floating above our heads.

We met at our therapist's office a few months back. When I saw him for the first time, I was instantly intimidated by his confidence in carrying such a disgraceful curse. He pompously sauntered about the ward, boasting about how many of his crimes weren't solved. He was throwing cigarettes on dry leaves to make nurses go nuts. He was a walking destruction, a great incendiary. Handsome, too. At that time, I was still secretive about my fantasies. Hidden in the closet.

"You're too pretty to have pyromania tendencies. Quite frankly, aren't you too pretty to even be here, or am I wrong?" he asked, looking at me with his eyes squinted. I wasn't sure whether I should take it as a compliment or a crude provocation.

"I've been to hell, you know. They were closed, so I had to come here instead," I answered calmly, while he just remained there, smiling at me. That's how our relationship began. Some may call it "love at first sight," but I prefer the term "a start of infernal incidents."

Throughout those months, we were driving across the country, committing small arsons with enormous enthusiasm and precision. It was the crucial factor to keep our passion fuming. The therapy sessions were rarely attended and, after a while, completely forgotten. We burned everything we could: from old photographs to dead animals. Furniture, small shops, computers, cars. We studied smells, smoke, and sounds. We perceived arson as the highest form of craftsmanship. And there we were, side by side, looking directly at our magnum opus. There was something off-putting, though. Burning autumn leaves and setting ancient forests on fire were two quite distinct things. I deeply knew that he was slowly going insane, but what was I to do about it? I simply loved him as he was. Finding someone who truly understood me was one thing, but finding someone who fully related to my ludicrous obsessions? A gift from the heavens. Once you get a rare bird like that, you have to put it in a cage and lock the cage shut.

"Exquisite time. Absolutely fantastic. I've never seen something like this before," he said grimly, lighting a cigarette and looking at the burning trees and buildings.

"Are you out of your mind?" I asked, slightly peeved at his irrational babble. I realized that even if this was our highest achievement, it was sinister. The only thing bothering me was how oblivious he was to the fact that at least a dozen cops must have been after us right then. How could he be so ignorant to the consequences of our actions? He put his pure ambition above everyone and everything else to reach the level of ancient gods who brutally played with innocent lives and destroyed them. I stared at him, at those dark blue eyes fueled with disturbing satisfaction hidden under blond curls. His face was paler than usual; he looked like a descendant of Dracula and Adonis, if they'd ever had one. And now this divine beauty had become a catalyst to our descent to Hades, or the ninth circle of Dante's hell.

Bright red sparkles flew into the asphalt skies. Trees aggressively swayed among the flames—reminiscent of William Turner's painting of London in 1666. As we stood there, looking at the art we'd made, a petrifying thought crossed my mind. He was filled with aplomb. He'd mastered the skill of manipulation. He possessed beauty, intelligence, and cunningness. If I wasn't a pyromaniac myself, he surely would've been able to find some silly, ingenuous girl who would be able to do the same things for him as I did, and maybe even more. I knew I wasn't enough, and I couldn't let him replace me. If my therapist had taught me one thing, it was that everyone is replaceable. There may have been another girl, as unhinged as I was, who could be easily charmed by this semi-god. Not after everything we've been through. No one could have my bird. No one could take him from my cage.

Deep down I knew what I had to do to make him stay with me forever. I grabbed a lighter from my left pocket and a flask filled with gasoline from my right.

She was everything I'd ever dreamt of. Since I saw her for the first time, sitting at the therapist's office, I knew it was no accident. She was perfect: beautiful, intellectual, and a pinch insane. I couldn't imagine anyone else in her place. She was a significant element of my complex plan. Purification by fire, the only way for eternal salvation. The fire that provided life and death equally. What mesmerized me the most was the possibility of entirely taking control over it, and she let those dreams transform into reality.

I'd always been fascinated with the mystical value of fire. I had a deep affection for it, but my love for her was above any of my fixations. Without her, none of this would be possible. Once she mentioned her arrival from hell the first time we met, I knew she'd been created for grand achievements. She was a muse that allowed me to metamorphose into my higher self. She helped me become a god, the second Prometheus.

I stood with my arms around her, trying to quell her trembling. I wondered whether it was because of her pride or pure fear of facing the consequences of our sin. We were playing gods, yet she was constantly mentioning the police and prison. I wasn't worried; anyone that had ever dared to challenge the gods ended up in eternal suffering. I took a longer look at her and started admiring every inch of her body. She was perfect, hellfire rising behind her. Her hazel hair waved to the rhythm of the night wind. She resembled an ancient goddess that had returned to Earth to seek revenge. And what a vengeance it was. I couldn't take my eyes off her; she was one of a kind, that's for sure.

"Consummatum est," I whispered, hypnotized by our work.

"Laeti vescimur nos subacturis," she responded, staring at the flames consuming the night. There was something uncanny in her eyes. Was it uncertainty? Distress? Annoyance? Whatever it was, it made me feel apprehensive. We were standing before our best creation, and yet she had the nerve to be dubious. That ought to be unforgivable at such a moment of triumph. The fire grew bigger and bigger, sizzling above us. The skies glowed red and orange, gradually disfiguring the view before us. For a split second, I felt doomed. Small. Fragile. That must have been how being in Pompeii felt like.

"Life was better before this moment," she suddenly declared with her eyes closed.

"What do you mean by that?"

"Well... we just achieved all that we've ever wanted. It can't get any better, *no*?"

She was right. There couldn't possibly be a larger goal than what we'd just achieved. And since our desired dream had finally come true, we had no clue what to do next. Nevertheless, her tone left me feeling anxious. What had she meant? Was our crime something that might divide us? I expected her to be in one of her mental states where she was lost, and it would get better soon. But what if it wouldn't? What if she, the person I cared about the most, decided to leave? Humans were full of surprises. Or worse, what if she found someone who could take my place, who could give her more excitement, more entertainment? The thought of someone else kissing her neck and holding her sent chills down my spine.

I couldn't let that happen.

I immediately started waging my options. Firstly, I rejected the idea of eliminating possible threats; that'd take too much time. Secondly, directly asking her could possibly scare her and make her think that I was slowly losing my mind, which would lead to her leaving me anyway. The third option lit up in my head like a revelation from the Almighty himself. What if there was an easy way to make her mine for eternity? By my side, unreachable for anyone at all. I reached for the back pocket of my jeans and felt a small cardboard box of matches. I'd bought them this morning. I took them quietly, and when her eyes trailed to a far-off distance, I lit one.

— — — — —

"Are you sure that's them? How can you tell from the remains?" Dr. Steiner asked Officer Fenn, both of them standing over the stack of bones, surrounded by dust and burnt trees. It was a rainy Monday morning; the sun was hidden behind gray clouds. The air was thick and smelled of autumn leaves and humidity.

"I'm pretty positive, but we need more proof to be sure. This blanket here, it's made of an expensive fireproof fabric. Come and take a look at the embroidery. What do you see?"

Dr. Steiner came closer to the officer and took the textile from his hands. The blanket was midnight blue, with hand-sewn initials embroidered with silver and golden thread in its corner.

"Those are the initials of my patients, but it may as

well be a coincidence, Officer. I haven't seen either of them in months."

"How many months, Dr. Steiner?" The tone of his voice became pitiful.

Dr. Steiner felt her stomach rising up to her throat. Blood was heating in her head, making it difficult to think straight. In spite of that, she somehow managed to collect herself and remain calm in the face of truth. Two of her patients had potentially just committed a terrible crime, and it was her fault. She shouldn't have let them leave.

"Eight. They stopped attending meetings, and I did not chase them. They were adults. I'm not responsible for their actions," she said, her voice slightly trembling. Officer Fenn saw that the doctor had started shuddering, either from the cold or fear.

"You don't have to worry, ma'am. You're not the one to blame for any of this. You won't face any charges. You'll only be needed as a witness."

"Tell that to the media."

They shared a silence, examining the ruins before them. Surprisingly, it was quite impressive how much destruction had been spread in such a short period of time. "You know," Fenn began steadily, "we've been looking for them for at least three months now. They'd been causing chaos wherever they went. Every time we'd reached the destination of their next possible target, they were always found somewhere else. We tried so hard to catch those bastards, but they were always two steps ahead of us. If there is anyone to blame for that, it's the police." Fenn grunted with a bitter tone.

Dr. Steiner was looking at the burnt tree limbs spread across the path to what had used to be the remains of the sacred ancient city.

"They did that to themselves?" she asked after a while, standing next to the bones, quivering.

"Precisely. I saw their papers in your office. Those kids were hella messed up, yet they managed to survive those eight months on their own. For others, it would've been impossible. It seemed that they even loved each other. What I wonder though, why shouldn't they help themselves, after the way they'd been treated?"

Dr. Steiner gave him a suspenseful look and handed him the blanket. She was exhausted by the heaviness of the guilt that was going to haunt her to the grave. She started walking away toward her car. It was time for her to leave. "Because all they were able to do was destroy each other, painfully, little by little."

Ethereal Scar

Isabella Fauber, New York

Reckless yet cautious
My heart was trapped in the hem of your pocket
The leaves turned an enticing
Scarlet hue as the brisk wind whistled against their fragile
branches
The water reflected the scene in distorted and
Contorted colors and shapes
I couldn't distinguish the different versions of myself
Blurred within the shallow water
In your eyes I lost a part of me in the hopes that I would
Be able to see

——

I was finally ready to fall
My only mistake was picking up your call
You shielded me from the cold
And warmed my frozen lips
It was only a kiss
So tell me why it hurts like this

Crestfallen

Hudson Warm, New York

Mother is fifty, but her face is without laugh lines; she doesn't laugh. Not since Father left. Mother stains her lips with crimson pigment that often smears on her teeth. Mother told Kora not to climb aboard the subway. Maybe she's overprotective because she doesn't want Kora to run away like he did.

The rusted silver beckons Kora forth, howling like a coyote on the edge of a cliff. Liquid pools left of her feet—water or urine, but she prefers naivety. The sliding doors glide open, providing a glimpse into the world Kora has never known. Broken silhouettes flash before her, disappearing into the bustle of the city.

Kora steps over the threshold and collapses into a stiff orange seat. It's not the velvet cushion she's used to, but it will do. It's her favorite in a different way. She keeps her eyes on her lap and picks at the white thread of her ripped jeans. The experience is sacred because Mother is unaware.

Muffled, foreign callings echo from the loudspeaker—words she cannot comprehend. Kora avoids the chewed gum to her left on the seat. At the next stop, a man in a yellow raincoat sits beside her before Kora can warn him about the gum that now sticks to his rear. She doesn't talk to him, just manages a stilted smile. Even that, she regrets immediately after.

At the next stop, a lady with black bobbed hair takes her other side. Two strangers flank Kora. The thin white strings of her ripped jeans are now broken.

It is not until the next stop that she completely lifts her gaze. Folding a brown skateboard under his arm, the boy seizes her attention. He looks to be seventeen or eighteen, close to Kora's age, with a floppy nest of brown waves that shouldn't be as striking as it is. Kora trails her eyes up and down his body, stopping at his pupils of sweet intent riddled with corruption. He returns the fierce gaze, and each of her bones contracts. His sweaty-looking palm is wrapped around a silver pole.

Kora flicks her eyes away and lets them catch on the rip in her jeans again. This time, she sketches an eye on her knee with her longest fingernail. Kora hasn't decided where she'll get off the subway. She hasn't decided on a stop. But now she decides she will get off when the captivating boy does.

Kora takes the mini notebook from the front pocket of her bomber and pens down a few thoughts—nothing eloquent enough that she'd want it written here. Someday she may offer it upon your eyes. She gets caught up in her inner monologue, so much so that when she looks up, the boy is gone.

Kora gets off at the next stop.

——

The subway is her newfound haven, her escape, her solace. Mother was screaming this morning. Kora forgets the words, just remembers they were there. Kora shut her creaky wooden door, but the shouts made their way through the faint crack between the wall and the door. Now she's stuck between two strangers in the third car of the subway.

Kora's stomach lurches as the subway halts, screeching against the tracks. It's only her second time, yet it feels so familiar. Like a dirty, infested, contaminated home. The sliding doors part, and a boy steps on, along with a cluster of other strangers. It couldn't be.

The doors meet again like two lovers and the world fades a little bit, all except for the boy. Same waves, same eyes, same palm wrapped around the same pole. Same car. Same stop. Same skateboard folded under the same armpit.

Same person.

His eyes meet hers with a flicker of recognition. "This has gotta be some sort of destiny." His voice isn't anything like Kora suspected. It's got a sullen edge to it that tells a story but leaves out the ending.

"You better not be a creepy stalker." The words escape her lips before she can think about what to say.

Some of the surrounding strangers glance up at them. A wrinkled woman smiles. A bearded man keeps his eyes glued to his phone.

"Don't worry. I'm not." He grins, and Kora sees his perfectly imperfect teeth. "What stop you getting off at?"

"Depends."

"On what?"

"Your answer to that same question."

The wrinkled old woman is probably smiling wider now, but Kora won't take her eyes off the boy.

The subway stops again and its doors part. The boy cocks his head to the entryway. "This one."

Kora rushes from her seat and follows, enclosed in his shadow. "Me, too."

The boy chuckles and slams his skateboard on the platform. One of his shoes is untied. He grunts faintly and hops on, despite the flurry of hurried bodies. "Where are we going?"

Kora checks her watch. She has a piano lesson back at home in twenty minutes. Mother would murder her. *Paris. Rome.* "You're the one who knows the area."

"Fair enough."

They share a companionable silence for the better part

of ten minutes—ascend the cement steps, avoid touching germy surfaces, let the air whip their faces. Kora opens her mouth to ask where they're going, then decides against it.

"Wanna try?"

"Pardon?" Kora meets the boy's eyes, which are crystals rimmed with brown.

"Skateboarding." He jumps off and lets the brown board wheel down the sidewalk. "Better go grab that before we lose it." A spark curves up the edges of his lips.

Kora grins and shakes her head, racing after the disappearing board. "I never caught your name," she manages between pants as she returns with the board in hand.

"True."

Kora furrows her brows at the mystery. "Are you gonna tell me?"

"When the time is right." His arms sit crossed in front of the chest of his navy blue tee. "Now come on, follow me. We're almost there."

Kora places one trembling foot on the board and waits for the boy to walk in front of her. She feels as if she knows both everything and nothing about him. He strides in a confident manner, with a level of self-assurance that Kora only wishes she could reach.

At once, he halts his saunter beneath a mustard-yellow awning. The sun gleams diagonally, falling like a blanket on his waves. "We're here."

Kora smiles when she thinks of Mother's current state: presumably furious, nervous, searching for her daughter.

Yesterday, Mother didn't realize Kora's disappearance; Mother had been on a walk with her personal trainer. She always seems to be with that personal trainer these days. Kora suspects that the title conveys only a slight, unimportant part of who he really is to Mother. She doesn't ask Mother about it because she doesn't quite care, and if she did, it wouldn't matter.

"You good?" asks the boy.

Kora flinches and regains her composure. He's holding the door open for her, and she wonders how long he's been standing there. "I'm perfect." She should feel suspicious of a stranger, but his jawline is sharp enough and his eyes are deep enough to distract her from the question.

A tall woman leads the two to a seat by the window, overlooking the streets astir. She flirts a smidge with the boy as she shows them to their table, and Kora feels strangely possessive of him. The woman expresses nothing verbally, but Kora thinks her body language speaks for itself.

"There is something troubling you again, isn't there?"

"Nothing at all," says Kora, now sitting across from the boy. Only now does she realize the stubble that decorates his cheeks. "Isn't it crazy that we just so happened to meet again on the subway today?"

"The chances are improbable, almost impossible," he agrees. "That's why I spoke up."

Kora orders a chai and the boy orders green tea. The

chai arrives in a transparent mug, so she can see the liquid falling after each sip like tears. It is a couple minutes past the start of her piano lesson now.

"Are you seriously not gonna tell me your name?" asks Kora.

"It's not like I know yours."

"Kora."

He hesitates. "That's pretty."

"It's your turn, now."

"You must give me time to think." The boy stares into his green tea as if it will give him answers.

"Why would you need to think long and hard about your name?"

"Well, I"—he flicks his gaze to the window, sunlight landing on his eyes through the panes—"I haven't yet decided what I want you to know me by."

Kora chuckles. "If you won't tell me, I'll just call you Conor, all right? You look like a Conor."

"Fine. One 'N' or two 'N's?"

"One, of course."

The boy retorts, "And with a C or a K?" as if the world depends on a single letter.

"My goodness, a C, of course."

"No, it has to be a K."

"Fine, Konor." Kora laughs. "How do you like your green tea?"

"It's not the most tasty, but I've heard it's good for you," he says.

"That's like a lot of things, isn't it?"

"I can't tell if you're saying that as a philosopher or a food critic," Konor says. "Either way, it's accurate."

"Well, if it is, I'd better get going."

"Fair enough." The boy takes another sip, scrunching his face at the steam that billows out. "This has been fun."

"It has."

"Tomorrow, same time, same car, same place?" asks Konor.

Kora nods, places a five-dollar bill on the hardwood surface, and scurries off.

—

When Mother smiles, she's either in love, or Father has returned. And Kora hasn't heard from Father in years, so the former seems to win.

"That personal trainer, isn't it?" Kora asks, lacing up her boots.

"How'd you know?"

"It was quite obvious."

"I'm sorry for not telling you." There is nothing apologetic in Mother's tone.

"Don't worry about it. I'm just glad you're happy again."

Mother ties her hair in a ponytail. Her lipstick is pink today instead of crimson. The lightness suits her better. "I'm going on a run. I'll be back to make you dinner, sweet pea." She's so oblivious that she doesn't even ask what Kora is up to.

"Mm-hmm, a run... What kind of run?"

"Kora!" she exclaims, glee lacing her voice. "I'll be back to make you dinner."

"Yes, you said that already."

Mother exhales. "Goodbye." She shuts the door lightly behind her, and Kora waits a couple minutes before opening that same door.

Today, she counts down the stops, seated on her trademark orange chair, fidgeting with her fingers, nervous for some reason. She alternates every few moments between clipping up her blond tresses to achieve an effortless portrayal and letting the locks run loose down her arms.

When the subway finally stops at Konor's station, Kora eyes a pasta advertisement on the wall, feeling heat rise to her cheeks in anticipation. She can't look too excited. She can't be staring right at him; that looked creepy when she practiced in her mirror last night.

But when the doors shut in what seems like slow motion, it doesn't matter if her hair is up or down, how excited she looks, that she is even there... Konor isn't coming. A dim glimmer of hope lurks; maybe he'll come on the next stop.

He never does.

Kora gets off at the same stop she did yesterday and walks in excruciating loneliness to nowhere. Absentmindedly. Fatigued. Yesterday was too good to be true, just like Mother always says of her and Father's early relationship.

After Father, Kora should've known not to believe promises. Kora remembers what Mother always says: *Men will let you down.* She detests listening to Mother, but from now on she just might. Because Mother would never do this to her: leave her crestfallen, descending a hill.

Get Away

Sophia Lind, New York
TW: Self-Harm

New York City makes me feel so alone yet more alive than I have ever felt. My uncle brought me here six months ago to finish high school and to help with the renovations of an abandoned hotel he'd just bought. He helped me get away from my family and the boring town of Georgetown, Texas, where I used to live, so helping him with the hotel is the least I could do. My uncle says he wants the hotel to be as "unique and eye-catching" as possible, and we are definitely achieving that.

My favorite room so far is the ballroom. The walls are cement with beautiful and intricate details and archways. Ivy is poking out of all the cracks in the walls, growing uncontrollably, and the ceilings are high with huge skylights and windows that let in all the afternoon sunlight, even on the darkest days.

My friend Sammy came up with the idea to paint all the walls in the ballroom to resemble their appearance in the rain. Huge wrinkled windows on every wall plaster shadows of the raindrops so beautifully throughout the room. The changing shadows make me feel small compared to what's around me. I come here a lot when I need to sort out my thoughts or simply get away from the world. I sit in the middle of the room, my knees curled into my chest, enchanted by the shadows transforming around me, immersing myself into a world that is finally my own.

Sammy is the only part of Texas that I truly miss. He's my best friend and, well, the only friend I felt I really had there. We always found our own ways of having fun when there was nothing to do in our lifeless town. We usually would hang out in Tattoos and Stuff, where he works, or eat at the diner across the street, where we would order our regular: French toast, sweet potato fries, and chocolate milk. We did everything together, from taking the same classes to trying to have a "normal" teenage life before we had to grow up. "Growing up" isn't exactly a concept I like to think about, especially after being told by my mother to "stop crying and grow up." This is one of her favorite sayings when I have an episode. I haven't seen Sammy in a while, and I sometimes think he was the only thing keeping me sane.

He came to visit me here once, and he had the same reaction as I did when I first walked into the ballroom. It was another rainy day, and the walls were covered by the same beautiful reflections of all the water droplets. His face immediately lit up, and he started twisting around in circles, trying to take everything in. He took out his sketchbook—it was always with him—and spent the rest of the day sketching every inch of the room. The artists even used his sketches as reference for when they painted the walls of the ballroom. Next, I showed him all the furniture that was left behind when the building was abandoned, and, not to my surprise, he sketched every piece. He told me that he loves things that are vintage, and he only draws things he loves. He filled up an entire sketchbook that weekend.

When I see these rooms, I don't just see "vintage;" I see all the people who were in these very rooms all those years ago, and I imagine what they would be doing if they were still here. There's furniture left in every room that has been collecting dust for decades. I think about the beauty that is being masked by filth, with no way to clean itself off and no sign of relief. I think about all the people who would rather throw them away, discarding all their hidden beauty, just to replace them with something new and without the comfort that comes with the old and familiar. My uncle agreed to keep the furniture as long as I figure out something to do with it that corresponds with the "theme" of the hotel.

— — — — — —

My uncle told me not long ago the whole story behind the hotel—why he wants it to be so "unique and eye-catching." It's all to find a lost love. At a family Christmas party seven years ago, he was exiled to New York when my family found out he was engaged to a man. His fiancé, Alec, never showed up at the airport to join him as he said he would. My uncle never saw or heard from him again, except for one letter.

Hector,

I want to be your husband so bad. I know that I shouldn't let other people's opinions of the two of us get in the way of that, but in all honesty, I'm terrified of what my family would think. You are so brave for what you did with coming out about us. I really wish I could do the same.

My family means everything to me, and I don't know how I could live without them in my life, and you know that. I need you to know that I love you more than anything, but now is not the time for us.

You have taught me so much about myself in the five years that we have been together, and I can't thank you enough for that. You made me feel things I never thought someone could, especially with a man.

Maybe one day we can be together again and have that wedding we have both been dreaming about. But I can't join you in New York, not yet, and I don't know when I can build up the courage to tell my family who I am.

I'm Sorry,
~ Alec

My uncle wrote letter after letter to Alec and sent them all to the apartment they shared in Texas. But with my uncle being in New York and Alec leaving out a return address on the letter, my uncle never got a response.

My uncle hopes tomorrow can be that one day that Alec talked about. He's advertising everywhere in and around Georgetown and anywhere else he can, spreading the news of the hotel. All of this to help make the grand opening as big as we can—to try to get Alec's attention, wherever he is.

My uncle has been there for me through all the ups and downs of my life before he left for New York. My parents often left me alone in my house, even when I was too young to take care of myself. My uncle would come over every time and pretend like everything was all right. Even now, after all the years of his separation from the family, he looks out for me like no one else has. When things become too much, he's the shoulder I go to and cry on.

In my eyes, he deserves to finally find his lost love, hence the furniture on the ceilings of the lobby. I know that sounds weird, but I found a use for those pieces of vintage furniture, and it gives the illusion that everything is upside down. We even installed a light on the floor to finish off the uniqueness of the room.

I had been helping the artists put the finishing touches on the lobby when I got a call. My mother is coming to the grand opening tomorrow. I haven't seen her since I left Texas, and I was planning on keeping it that way, or at least for a while longer. I should have expected she would hear about it from all the publicity it's already getting in anticipation.

"Cleaning up your apartment before I get there wouldn't be such a bad idea," she told me over the phone. "I know how you are, and since I am a *guest* now, it's the right thing to do, Tobin." She ends the call before I can say anything else.

My heart is beating so fast, I can hear it in my chest and feel it in my ears. Getting away has never been enough to free me of her control. I drop my paintbrush and rush out of the hotel. No one needs to see me like this.

It's raining outside, and only then do I remember I forgot to take an umbrella, classic. Through the clouds, the sun is lighting up the city. Looking up as the drops of rain hit my face makes me smile, and I can no longer remember any of my thoughts. One moment of serenity and relief is just what I needed.

A woman shoves herself into me, not giving a second look or a moment of sorriness as she continues down the street. I'm back to floating alone, above all these people who are living their lives without giving a second thought about mine.

A busy city can still be lonely.

All the bottled-up emotions I have been suppressing catapult back into my mind. Every inconvenience, every moment of inconsistency and invisibility is adding weight on my shoulders. My feet are dragging behind me, making it more and more difficult to move forward. Standing at the crosswalk, I feel as if I will combust if I wait for even another second. Anxiety heats up and rushes to all the ends of my body, forcing sparks from my fingertips that can't stop until I get to my apartment. I walk across the street; a car is coming toward me from my left, another swerves to my right, and another stops abruptly, throwing everything forward in the car, stopping only a few feet from me. My eyes stay glued to the ground as I run the rest of the way.

I get to my building, continuing to run toward the elevator. I think the landlord is trying to talk to me, but I don't have time to listen. The elevator door closes behind me, and I feel eyes on me. I search every corner as I get closer and closer to reaching the fourth floor, my floor.

A hand is on my back. Whose hand? No one's with me in this elevator. A few steps to the center of the elevator, turning in circles, no crevice left uninvestigated. Still, no one's here.

Tears stream down my face. I'm gasping for every breath. I have no control over my body. My hands, they appear strange to me. I'm looking down at my feet but from a distance, a distance much larger than my five-foot-seven" body. The reflection on the door shows a stranger looking back at me. I know it's me, but I don't feel any sort of attachment to it. Someone's pressing their body against my back, slowly stretching their arms around me, squeezing. In my reflection, I'm still alone.

Uncontrollably shaking legs are underneath me. They're mine, but without any connection to the rest of me. My hands move back and forth. I try and I try to see things from my own eyes. Everything is different; nothing is my own. It is as if a new lens has been placed on how I see things, and it hasn't been able to focus yet.

I'm scratching at the skin on my fingers, trying to feel something, but it's as if the nerves in my arms aren't mine, and I am feeling all these things still from a distance.

The elevator door opens, and I run without looking back. I run through the long, twisty, green-painted hallways that lead me to what is always mine. I can't get there fast enough. My chest rises and falls faster now, but I can't feel my breaths. I fumble with the keys in the shaking hand in front of me, the hand that is hardly mine.

I have had moments like this ever since I was five, and it's never stopped. Almost every time, I find myself on the bathroom floor. I'm not surprised to find myself here again.

Crouched over in the corner of the room, head in my hands. My eyes try to close, but I quickly open them again. I'm too afraid of leaving myself vulnerable. I'm crying and breathing too fast to catch up. I want to recognize myself again. I want the pain in my chest, in my head, in my stomach to stop. It all needs to stop.

My eyes open. I still can't see straight. What's that noise? Oh, right—I started a bath. Why did I start a bath?

Touch the water four times. The water's hot. My hand's burning. *Three more or you die in the next four minutes.* Maybe the water isn't so bad. Pain is just a feeling, right?

The mirror is fogging up. I should clean it off, but I don't want to use a towel; it will drag over the sink. *The sink has germs.* I clean them off, but there will always be some left behind that I haven't been able to get to.

Touch the sink sixteen times. The sink is almost dry. I guess I brushed my teeth a while ago. *Or did you? Your teeth could be dirty from crying. Brush them again or they'll all fall out.* Did I brush my teeth? My gums hurt. My gums are bleeding. I probably just need a new toothbrush.

The tub overflows. I guess I forgot about it. I wonder how long I've been here for. *Check the time as many times as you can without it changing.* 10:20 p.m., 10:20 p.m., 10:20 p.m., 10:20 p.m., 10:21 p.m.

"Shit!" *Run to your bedroom and back four times in the next four seconds or you die. You already messed up the last one. You don't have any other options.* I thought I got to my apartment while it was still daytime. Where did those hours go? What have I been doing all this time?

Jump in the full bathtub or you die. The water is still scalding, but I'd rather burn myself again than die.

"Ow!" I hit my head on the side of the tub. My blood dyes the water red around me. I'm fine. Anything other than dying. I'm being dramatic. It didn't hurt that bad. I could handle worse.

I'm hungry. *Cut something within four seconds or you will never eat again.* One Mississippi... Two Mississippi... Three Mississippi... Four. I made it. I sit for a moment to catch my breath. Running to my kitchen and finding a knife in four seconds isn't so easy. My body is dripping wet; I didn't have enough time to dry off or to put clothes on.

Run each of your fingers across the blade sixteen times or cut your wrists. I don't want to cut myself. Better my fingertips than anywhere else, I guess.

The blood runs farther down my body. Sammy calls. I still have eight more rounds to go. *Run to your bedroom in four seconds without saying a word.* I wonder what it would feel like to run the knife down my arm. I shouldn't think that. *Run the knife down your arm four times or add pressure.*

Lucky for me, Sammy is on a tangent, so I add a "yea" or "I totally agree" every few seconds. That keeps him talking. I'm still crying, but I've gotten better at calming my voice after all these years of hiding these breakdowns.

I make it to my room, and finally I can put some clothes on. My hands are shaking, making it difficult to pull my shirt over my head. *Come on, eight more times across your fingers. You saw what it was like to have to slit your wrist.* My fingers start to bleed. My wrists start to bleed. *Go to sleep right now. Don't open your eyes again until it is bright outside. Do you want to see what lurks in the dark?*

What have I done to deserve this? I want to open my eyes. But I can't, so I hang up on Sammy. I'll try to survive.

I wake up and dried tears stain across my face. I drag myself out of bed. I left a mess behind yesterday. The bathtub is full of red water, and the floor is covered with it. I can't remember starting a bath. I must have forgotten about it then, too. Through my door, I see the knife I left on the kitchen counter and blood still dripping from the table to the floor.

"Ow." I pull my hand away from myself and see the cuts on all my fingers. I can barely remember cutting my fingers. My bed is stained red. I'm crying again. I am so exhausted that I collapse and cover my face, lying on the floor, legs bent and limbs extending in all directions. Pulling away one of my hands from my face, I feel the dry blood that has traveled down my back from a cut on the back of my head. Then I see the cuts going down my arms.

Removing my other hand, I see my face in my mirror in front of me. My eyes are swollen, and red blotches cover my face. I recognize myself; I just wish it wasn't me. I drag myself off the floor and look closely into my reflection, breaking down again. I watch as tears fall more quickly than I can stop them. I study my face, and I smile. I smile as big as I can to make sure I still can when I see my mother later.

I don't have to be happy to smile, do I?

I pull myself together to the point where it is unnoticeable what happened last night. I clean up my apartment and cover up the cuts on my arms with makeup, hiding the things no one needs to know. Another call, this time from my uncle telling me to come to the hotel early. Something about wanting help to set up the tables for the guests' first meal tonight.

Later that night, while making my way around the lobby and introducing myself to the first guests, I find him. Sammy. He's standing by the door holding a bag. Even from across the room, I can tell he's holding French toast, sweet potato fries, and chocolate milk. I'm running over to him, accidently pushing myself through the crowd to wrap my arms around him. He tells me how he was worried about how I ended our call last night, so he is here to surprise me and catch up.

Where we are by the door makes it impossible to hear each other or stand without getting shoved by guests still filtering in. I make my way around the first floor; I have to find my uncle and say goodnight so Sammy and I can head to my apartment and talk.

Walking into the ballroom, I immediately notice the walls. They really do capture what I see on rainy days. My eyes trace over the walls where I could so easily get lost in the shapes and colors. But I need to find my uncle. The room is full, but he is easy to pick out of a crowd; he likes to say it's something about his energy that is "irresistible."

He's dancing in the center of the room with a man I don't recognize. From the light in both of their eyes and the smile on my uncle's face, I can tell he found Alec. I turn back to Sammy, and we head to my apartment before I can interrupt.

I open the door to my place. I know the conversation I'm about to have with Sammy; might as well get it over with so we can enjoy the rest of this night.

I turn to see Sammy's reaction to my place, but he's not smiling—Sammy's always smiling—as he looks past me. I turn toward my kitchen; my mother is standing before me. I never gave her a key, but I can't say I'm surprised that she found a way in. She looks up at me but doesn't move from where she stands over my sink. Her arms are resting on either side of it, and she has a look on her face that I have never seen from her. She's worried.

My heart drops as I walk over to her. Peering down into my sink, I know what's about to happen. Quickly, I look back to her, then to Sammy.

The knife I cut myself with last night sits in the sink, unwashed.

"I knew it was bad, Tobin, but what is this? Are you cutting yourself now?" My mother glances down at my wrists where the makeup has worn off. I walk into my bedroom, alone, and lie down.

I thought I could hide this part of myself. I never wanted anyone to worry. There's nowhere left for me to get away to now.

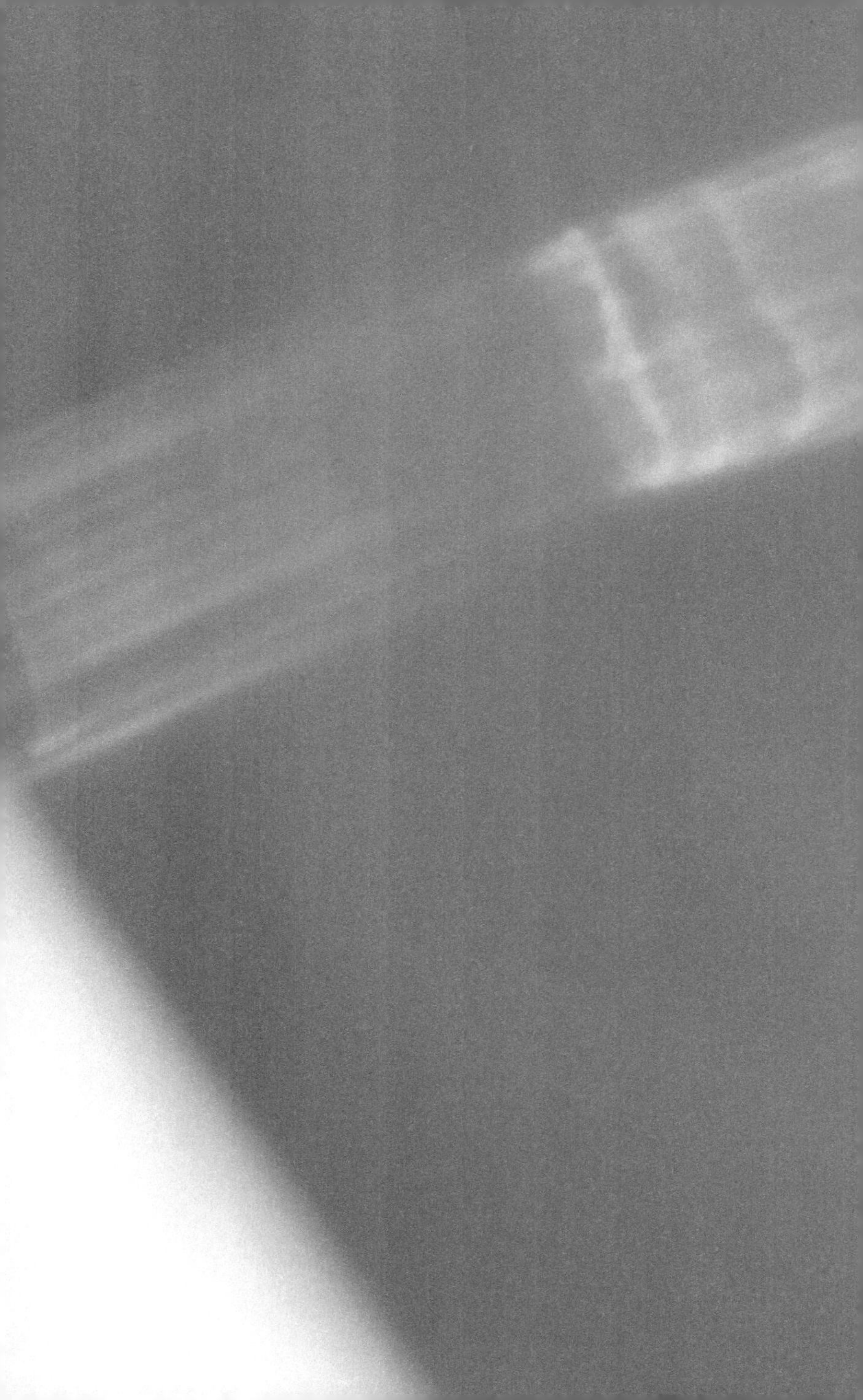

NIGHT.

NIGHT.

That Night

Heather Kirchhoff, Missouri

In one moment everything changed.
I watched my life shatter before my eyes.
I watched my hope fade away as glass broke.
Buildings crumbled to the ground.
My home vanished before my eyes.
My mom's promise rang in my ears.
"I'll come back."
So where are you now?
Silvery tears descended on my cheeks.
I watched as my village burned,
As the flames flickered in the still night, devouring,
Wrecking everything for me.
Flames jumped, mocking me.
The smoke tumbled into the dark night sky.
My aunt held me as screams echoed.

—　—

Coldness seeped into me.
I shivered, unable to control it.
My body quivered slightly,
With a tingling sensation.
Pain shot through my head, pulsing from the back of my
skull.
I was immobile. Stuck.
A voice repeated,
"You are mine."
My eyes darted around the room
Then rested on
The mirror on the far wall.
I gasped at my reflection.
Horror crept up on me, stealing my breath.
My eyes weren't their usual blue.
They were red,
Glistening with the need to kill.

The Boy and His Cat

MC Pending, Florida

Harmony Greigh was an average fourteen-year-old girl, with an average life, an average family, and average grades. That was, until the summer she spent at her grandparents' house.

Harmony was very against the idea. It was a five-hour drive, and she and her brother Julian barely even knew their grandparents. CeCe and Gramps never visited on Christmas or Thanksgiving. They never seemed to leave Arizona, and Harmony had only been to their mansion once many summers ago, before her parents got divorced and she started spending the summers in Florida with her dad. But Dad was busy this summer, so Mom was determined to make Harmony suffer through six weeks of grandparents and nonstop brother.

"Kids! We're here!" Mom called, slowing the minivan. Harmony looked up from her sketchpad and out of the car window. The van pulled up to an enormous house. They rolled to a stop on a light concrete driveway so clean that Harmony wondered if anyone had ever driven on it before.

"Wow." Julian gasped, pressing his face against the car window, fogging it up with his astonished breaths and handprints. Harmony craned her neck, peering around her brother.

Wow, was about right. The house was huge.

"I bet you could fit a whole spaceship inside!" Julian giggled, squishing his nose against the glass.

Harmony rolled her eyes and pulled out her AirPods, quickly changing her mind and reinserting them as Julian began asking Mom an unending list of rather stupid questions.

Mom stayed quiet as she parked the car and hopped out. She rushed around, opening the trunk and unloading suitcases. Harmony sighed heavily, stuffing her sketchpad into her backpack and opening the van door. Slowly, she made her way to the back of the car to help Mom. Julian was apparently too busy gaping at the house through the window to realize Harmony was unloading his suitcase, even though she didn't have to.

Mom pulled out one of Harmony's AirPods, pausing the music. She stared at her daughter for a long moment before tucking a strand of Harmony's chestnut hair behind her ear.

"I know this isn't the ideal summer," Mom said with an encouraging smile, "but try to have fun. Your grandparents love you very much, and I think you're going to have a great time."

"Mom! I dropped my Switch between the seats!" Julian cried from inside the van.

"And take care of your brother for me," Mom added, wrinkling her nose.

Harmony rolled her eyes again, putting her AirPod back in her ear as Mom went to Julian's aid. All the suitcases were out on the driveway, and Harmony had just pressed the button to close the van's trunk when Julian finally appeared.

Together, the three of them approached the front door of the mansion. Mom helped pull Julian's rolling suitcase up the porch steps, one hand on her son's shoulder.

"Remember your manners," Mom said.

"Yeah, okay," said Julian, practically bouncing with excitement.

Mom cleared her throat, which to a passerby might have seemed normal but to Harmony was as good as a death threat.

"I mean yes ma'am!" Julian corrected himself. "Now can I ring the doorbell? I bet it's fancy!"

Mom sighed, ruffling his dark hair. But CeCe opened the door before Julian even got to ring the doorbell.

"Oh Nova!" Harmony's grandmother exclaimed, embracing Mom warmly. CeCe was as tall as Mom. She looked a lot like her too, except while Mom's hair was almost black, CeCe had short pure white hair. Very grandmotherly. But both Mom and CeCe shared the bright blue eyes Harmony had always wished for.

Mom broke the hug, saying something Harmony couldn't quite hear. CeCe only smiled, eyes drifting to her grandchildren and house guests for the next six weeks.

"My my, Harmony! You've grown three feet since I saw you last!" CeCe said, grabbing Harmony's shoulders and looking her up and down. Harmony gave a curt nod and an awkward smile.

CeCe turned and called into the house, "Old man! Your grandchildren are at the door! Get down here before I put thumbtacks in your chair!" And then with a chuckle she turned back to Harmony. "Come in, come in. Your grandfather will be down in a moment." CeCe stepped back, pushing the door wide open.

Harmony followed Mom inside, who quickly snagged her AirPods again and warned her to put them away. CeCe caught Julian on his way in, plastering a grandmother-sized kiss on his cheek. Harmony was glad she was too old for kisses.

The interior of the house was incredible: a huge living room, a library the size of Harmony's house in San Diego, a kitchen the size of China, and at least five visible cats roaming around.

Great, Harmony thought. *CeCe is a crazy cat lady.*

After another threat from CeCe, Gramps came huffing down the stairs and into the kitchen. Mom smiled big when she saw him, and then they hugged for like a whole minute. Gramps was very tall, even taller than Mom and CeCe, who were both already a sturdy height. Other than being so big, Gramps was a typical grandfather. He had gray hair and glasses that rested on his nose. His eyes were like Harmony's: a soft caramel brown; but, unlike hers, his eyes radiated with happiness. He grinned from ear to ear as he tousled up Harmony's hair.

"Oh, if it isn't Huckleberry and Snulian!" Gramps mused.

"Those are not our names!" Julian exclaimed, placing his hands on his hips.

"Oh, silly me. It's been so long, I must have forgotten… It's Haley and Jacob, right?" Gramps decided. Harmony knew he was joking, but Julian was taking it quite seriously.

"No! *I'm* Julian, and *that's* Harmony!" he demanded, pointing at his big sister. Harmony rolled her eyes, while Gramps raised his eyebrows in mock surprise.

"Oh, that's right," he said, earning the soft laughter of CeCe.

"Your gramps is very old and forgetful and needs a nap," CeCe said. "Since I'm much younger and much stronger, I'll never forget your name. But we must forgive him, please, Julian. He can't help it after all."

"Okay," Julian said, hugging Gramps.

"Well, I'd better be off," Mom interrupted, one hand on each of her children's shoulders. Julian latched on to her leg, grumbling about how six weeks was a long time.

Harmony was hoping that Mom might stay, at least for dinner, but she seemed to leave at her first chance. The five of them made their way back out of the house and onto the porch, where two swift hugs were all the goodbyes.

"Call me every night!" Mom shouted from the van. And then she waved, rolled up the window, and was gone. Just like that, Harmony's already boring life got a little dimmer.

"Why don't you two pick your rooms while I get supper ready? Gramps will show you upstairs," CeCe suggested, hand on Harmony's back.

Harmony reluctantly obeyed and hauled her suitcases up the spiral staircase behind Gramps. All she really wanted was to be alone and maybe listen to some music and draw. But Gramps certainly didn't seem like he wanted her to be alone, and he definitely didn't want her to suffer from some peace and quiet.

"So, Harmony Roselyn Greigh, what have you been up to lately?" Gramps questioned in between rooms.

Harmony grimaced. She hated it when people used her middle name.

"Nothing," she replied dismissively.

"Nothing? You've been doing nothing since I saw you last?" Gramps asked. Julian laughed beside him. Harmony closed her eyes for a second in order to keep from rolling them, and then she shrugged.

"That's what most teenagers do, isn't it?" she mumbled.

She'd heard the *you do nothing around this house* talking-to way too often. At this, Gramps chuckled.

"So anyway, how's your boyfriend?" he prodded. Julian laughed again, knowing Harmony's answer would embarrass her.

The only luck Harmony had ever had with boys ended with the school semester and a prettier, blue-eyed girl.

"He's not very fond of being nonexistent, but I'm sure he's used to it by now," Harmony said. She was not amused with her grandfather's never-ending questions; it reminded her all too much of Julian.

"Why do you have so many cats?" Julian inquired, stooping over to pet an orange tabby that had caught his attention. The feline hissed at him and scurried away, taking cover between Gramps's legs.

"Your grandmother and I rescue them and find them better homes. If nobody wants them, we keep them." Gramps replied.

Even better, thought Harmony. *Both her grandparents were crazy cat people.*

"Gramps, do you have an Xbox?" Julian asked.

"It is my firm belief that you might just be able to survive six weeks without your brain-melting activities," Gramps explained, pulling at the bottom of his shirt.

"No Xbox?" Julian gasped. "What do you do all day?"

After the half-hour tour, Harmony picked one of the bigger rooms, completely coincidentally across the house from the one that Julian picked. It contained a twin bed and huge windows that gave her a nice view of her grandparents' landscape. It was neatly decorated with glow in the dark stars on the ceiling, a painting of the starlit sky, and a desk covered in art supplies in the far corner. She wouldn't have admitted it aloud, but Harmony kind of liked her room.

Harmony sat on the twin bed, staring at the starry ceiling. She wondered if another teenage girl had lived in this room before her. If so, she hoped that girl's life went better than her own.

CeCe called for supper soon after Harmony had finally put in her earbuds, and with a begrudging sigh, she slid off her bed and slowly made her way downstairs.

Harmony ate in silence, partially listening to Julian's questions and partially wondering how long six weeks would last. When everyone was finished, Gramps announced that he was going to tell a story. Harmony got comfortable on the couch by a window, watching the sunset.

"This story is my and CeCe's favorite," Gramps said, stealing a mischievous glance at CeCe, who sat beside him. She smiled.

"I like to call it, *The Boy and His Cat*," he said.

"It should be named after the girl, but go ahead, honey," CeCe muttered.

Harmony rolled her eyes, uninterested. She'd have

rather been up in her room listening to her music than listening to Gramps try to tell a story.

Her grandfather seemed to notice her distaste and gifted her with a clear-eyed look through his glasses that suddenly made Harmony feel weirdly guilty. She quickly shrugged away the emotion, and Gramps began his story.

——

A long time ago, before you were born, before your parents were even born, a dirty grimy boy named Lucas prowled the streets. He was a thief, with no family except his faithful black cat. The boy's brown eyes and hair matched the dirt-smudged clothes he wore. He was quite handsome under some layers of grime. But, I say, there were a lot of layers of grime.

Lucas liked to steal money from those who had plenty to spare. He often thought of himself as a sort of Robin Hood. *Steal from the rich and give to the poor*, he'd say, the rich being whoever kept their wallets in their pockets and the poor being himself.

But lately, Lucas wasn't feeling like a very good thief. He had the skills, but he lacked the lack of conscience. It was worse enough being insecure about your only occupation, but his cat, Noir, teased him about it.

His cat teased him? you might ask. Yes. His cat poked fun at him all the time.

The boy had just snagged a stale piece of bread from an unguarded bench when a peddler caught his eye.

"Look at that, buddy," he said to Noir, who was perched on his shoulder, and the black cat turned his head. "That peddler seems to have junk from all over the place."

On the contrary, Noir wasn't interested in the peddler at all, since he wasn't selling food or mirrors, but the remains of Lucas's bread caught his eye. The cat sniffed hungrily, forgetting that Lucas had already given him a healthy share and more.

Lucas mistook his furry friend's disinterest as a challenge. "You don't think I can do it?" Lucas smirked, eyeing the poor peddler. "I bet he has something we can snag and sell. If I could just get a closer look..."

A crowd had gathered, and pushing through the horde of people was someone Lucas recognized. And cringed at the sight of. The man was rich and crabby, and a figure Lucas had stolen from an exceptional amount of times. (He couldn't help it. I mean, the man was *loaded*.) Luckily, the man, called Mr. Gredihans, was preoccupied and took no notice of the boy and his cat in the alley.

Lucas's attention was drawn by Noir snagging the piece of bread from his hand and leaping off of his shoulder and onto a crate.

"Hey!" Lucas shouted. The cat gave him a look that seemed to say, *It's mine now, sucker*. And with that, Noir turned his back to the boy.

"You filthy, greedy, pig of a cat!" Lucas scowled, but he

really didn't mind at all. He was simply a great actor. "I'll just go and rob someone without you," he decided loudly, stealing a glance at his friend.

Noir took no notice, neatly nibbling on the bread and obviously taking his time. The cat earnestly enjoyed the practice of ignoring the boy. Lucas shot his eyes up to heaven and then heaved himself to his feet, pushing his attention back to the crowd.

A line had formed, and Mr. Gredihans was at the front. The peddler was trying to convince the rich man to buy some sort of metal staff. The staff was quite beautiful, made with tender care by a gifted craftsman.

Lucas gasped at the amount of coins Mr. Gredihans gave the peddler in return for the staff. *If I can sell it for that much, I'll be eating a week's worth of food every day*, Lucas thought hungrily before adding, *if Noir doesn't eat it all first.*

It wasn't hard for Lucas to follow Mr. Gredihans. The man was whistling loudly, elated with his newest purchase. Briefly, Lucas wondered what exactly the peddler had told Mr. Gredihans about the staff. Maybe it was a nobleman's from a century back, or perhaps it was crafted with the gentle hands of an ancient queen. Either way, Lucas would be happy with its worth.

So the boy snatched the staff the moment Gredihans put it down and was back into the safety of the alleys before the rich man could even blink. Noir had found his way back to his boy companion. He leapt nimbly from crate to crate, arriving to inspect Lucas's prize.

"She's a beauty, isn't she?" Lucas said in awe, turning the staff over and over in his hands.

Noir gave an unimpressed meow.

"No, you can't *eat* it," Lucas said, tapping the staff on the ground. "It's like a cane. A walking stick." He hunched over like an old man, demonstrating the staff's purpose for Noir.

The cat blinked.

"Don't ask me," Lucas murmured. "I don't know why it's so special! I just know that we can sell it for enough money to eat all the bread in the world."

Noir perked up at the sound of food.

Lucas remembered that he was hungry and that Noir had stolen his lunch. He leaned the staff against a crate in order to grab an apple he'd left inside a neighboring crate. He abandoned the staff for only a moment, but in that moment, Noir managed to tip it over. It teetered, and then it slammed against the pavement, splitting in half.

"Noir!" Lucas cried, hands in his hair as he stared at the broken staff. He turned to reprimand the cat, but Noir was already gone, hiding from the boy. "This is what I get for having a black cat. You unlucky little—"

Lucas bent, reaching for the staff, when both the pieces started rolling away. Before he could even react, a sudden beam of light and a screech from Noir welcomed a girl, appearing from inside the staff itself.

She was stunning. A long white braid ran down her

back. It faded into a bright blue color at the ends, nearly matching her unsettlingly piercing gaze. Her face was ethereal, an otherworldly sort of beauty, though her mouth was set in a stern line. Any spectators could come to the conclusion that she was foreign, due to the ragged and strange clothes she wore and her unique hair color.

Lucas stared aghast at the girl for what seemed like an hour as she returned the stare harshly. There was no ounce of friendliness in her icy blue eyes. He began to feel a teensy bit unsafe as her gaze grew colder and colder.

"Hello there?" Lucas croaked finally, offering half a wave.

The strange girl ignored his greeting completely and turned away from him, her eyes settling upon the staff. She stretched out a hand. She didn't even have to stoop over to retrieve it. The staff literally flew into her grasp.

Lucas started to feel a little more unsafe and, admittedly, a little flabbergasted. It was then that Lucas saw that the staff had not broken, but only slid apart, forming two blades.

The girl shoved the blades back together with a screech of metal, reforming the staff. She looked around, angry at the alleyways. And then she just walked away.

"Hey!" Lucas shouted, scrambling after the girl. "Hey! Wait! That's my staff!" He trotted to keep the girl in sight but wisely kept a measurable distance between them. The staff had, quite miraculously, flown into her hands. He had no way of telling what else the girl could do, but he wasn't just about to give up a week's worth of food every day. At least not without giving it five more minutes.

"Hello?" Lucas called after her. "I'd like that staff back, and then I'll just be on my way."

The girl turned on her heel and faced him, glaring so intensely Lucas wondered if she was going to scream at him or chase him or something. As the shivers ran down his spine, he found reason in not having a week's worth of food every day.

"This staff," she said, pointing it at him. "Is *not* yours." The girl's voice was low and eerie, edged with a thorough warning. She turned her nose up to him and marched away.

Lucas stared after her, dumbstruck. Watching from a nearby crate, Noir purred, as if content with the boy's despair.

"Oh shut up." Lucas groaned, shooting the cat an annoyed look. "It's your food, too."

Noir's pink tongue lolled over his paw, his green cat eyes blinking smugly at the boy.

"You unlucky garbage rat," Lucas growled, before sprinting after the girl, calling, "Hey, wait up!"

Some might say that Lucas followed the girl to take back the staff, but he was really following her to see where she'd go. She had literally appeared from inside the staff somehow, despite the great size difference, and the boy was starting to wonder who this girl was.

Lucas also knew that if Mr. Gredihans found the girl with the staff that he had stolen, she would not be welcomed with smiles. Gredihans had a reputation for shaking up anyone who got in his way. And Lucas, despite having to steal for a living, wasn't the kind of boy that would let the girl suffer for something she didn't do.

It wasn't hard for Lucas to follow the girl with the staff. She was obviously lost in the alleys that he had memorized years ago. Eventually, he caught up with her, having cornered herself for the seventeenth time in the labyrinth of alleyways.

"Hi. It's me again," said Lucas, leaning against the wall. He readjusted his hand placement a couple times, wondering if she was ever going to turn around. *Why was he so nervous?* He cleared his throat.

"I know you're probably lost, and you probably still want to kill me, but I know my way around. And I know there are some people out there that really want that staff." *Including me.* "So it would be unwise, truly a catastrophe, for you to refuse my assistance."

The girl pivoted, long braid whipping around over one shoulder. She glared coldly at her pursuer, gripping the staff so hard Lucas started to think she might just crush it.

"This is not my home," she said after a long time, icy gaze softening slightly.

"Ya think?" the boy murmured under his breath before replying, "And where, might I ask, is home?"

The girl turned her gaze to the darkening sky and pointed the staff toward the stars. "Beyond," she said simply.

"Beyond," Lucas echoed, stuffing his hands in his pockets. "That's right. *Beyond.* I've heard of it. Just past Wonderland on the left."

The girl looked at him again, lowering her staff. She seemed to contemplate the accuracy of his words.

After a couple moments of being scanned by her scary eyes, he wondered if he should mention that the Wonderland thing was a joke.

"Why am I here?" asked the girl, brows furrowed slightly.

"Your guess is as good as mine," Lucas said, running a hand through his hair. "I dropped the staff and BOOM! A girl with really long white-and-blue hair appears. I don't know what daily rituals go on in *Beyond*, but here, that doesn't usually happen," he said, stepping a little closer.

"*You*," the girl said, voice growing fierce.

Lucas regretted his decision to step closer very quickly. He felt the color drain from his face as she approached him. She lifted the staff, pointing directly at his face.

Lucas backed into the wall, but the girl kept coming. And where was his dang cat? The boy didn't feel like getting murdered all by himself.

"You brought me here," said the girl. "You will bring me home."

Lucas frowned. He hadn't exactly signed up to transport girls to and from magic staffs and "Beyond." But something about the staff's pointy end and the girl's firm stance made him very wary about saying no.

Noir, on the other hand, purred delightedly as the girl threatened Lucas's life. The cat was perched on a small balcony, head between the railing and tail swaying contentedly as he watched the boy. And though Lucas wanted to curse his friend, the cat's mischievous eyes reminded him that the girl still had the staff. Lucas could snag it from her at any moment if he gained her trust. And then he could vanish, sell the staff, and get fat off of a week's worth of food every day.

The girl was still waiting. She didn't notice the cat.

"Fine." Lucas sighed, shifting the staff away from pointing at his chest with a finger.

The girl appeared relieved, though she yanked the staff away from him. Perhaps her trust would prove a challenge to win. A challenge may be a challenge, but a pretty girl is a pretty girl.

"What's your name?" he inquired, tugging at the bottom of his shirt.

The girl didn't answer him at first, but eventually she said, "They call me Seafrost."

"*Seafrost?*" Lucas couldn't help but laugh. Sure, she came from a staff, but who has a name like Seafrost? She had to be joking.

The girl frowned.

"You're serious?" Lucas gulped, bottling his hysteria. "Can I call you Frosty?"

The girl turned away from him, headed back down the alleyway.

"You're fast." Lucas huffed, jogging after her. "Aren't you going to ask me what my name is?" When met with silence, he mumbled, "It's Lucas, by the way." And then he made a dangerous move, linking his arm with hers and careening down another street, the very one he lived on.

Seafrost recoiled, snapping her arm away from him, but she followed him anyway. The shade was lengthening as the day wore on, shielding them from the sun.

"Welcome to my humble abode," Lucas said as they arrived at his crate, sweeping his arms toward the dump of a place.

Seafrost looked unimpressed.

"What? You guys don't live in boxes in 'Beyond?'"

"They are nice... boxes," she said, furrowing her brows. Lucas hid his smile.

"This is just a rental," Lucas said, patting his crate and playing proud. "I'm staying here while I save up to buy a castle." He elbowed the dumpster to his left, and four or five rats skittered out from underneath.

Seafrost watched as the rodents took cover in a mound of garbage.

"Nosy neighbors," Lucas said.

Noir sensed the boy's show-off attitude and decided that he wanted to impress the staff girl, too. So the cat leapt down onto Lucas's shoulder and bit his ear.

Seafrost jumped, snapping the staff up in defense. And then she jabbed, only missing Lucas and the cat by centimeters.

"Whoa, whoa, whoa, whoa," Lucas cried, hands held up in surrender. Noir was barely holding on, clawing the boy's brown hair to keep from slipping to the ground.

"You are being attacked!" Seafrost said, obviously confused.

"He's my friend!" cried Lucas, scooping up Noir and cradling him like a baby. "He's harmless. An arrogant little termite." Noir screeched in protest, disgusted and utterly embarrassed to be in the boy's arms in the presence of a pretty stranger.

Seafrost lowered her weapon, even more confused.

"Frosty, meet Noir." Lucas released the black ball of fury, who hissed and then scrambled off to hide between crates.

"What is that?" Seafrost wondered, staring after the bitterly humbled Noir.

"*He* is a cat. And a thorn in my side."

"A cat?" she repeated.

Lucas looked up to see the faintest trace of a smile on the girl's face. A fluttering sensation filled his chest, but he quickly pushed away the feeling.

"So, anyway, can I take a look at your staff? Maybe it holds the key to how I can get you back to your world," Lucas suggested, holding out his hands.

Seafrost gripped the staff harder and shook her head.

"You will take it and run," she accused.

Maybe she's not as oblivious as I hoped, Lucas thought as she unknowingly recited his exact plan.

"Whaaat? No..." Lucas murmured, lowering himself onto a crate. Seafrost mimicked him, resting the staff in between her knees and watching him with undisguised distrust. The boy wondered if she'd try to stab him if he snatched the staff. He also wondered how fast she could run. Finding himself in the middle of a staring contest, Lucas decided he didn't want to find out.

"So," Lucas said, finally glancing away. He wrung his wrists, trying not to look at her and failing. "You get out much?"

Seafrost turned her nose up. "How is sitting on your boxes and talking to each other helping me get home?"

"Trust the process, Frosty. I know what I'm doing." Lucas did, in fact, know what he was doing. Stalling. That's what he was doing.

Noir crept out of the shadows, peering innocently at Seafrost. His tail was raised, and Lucas swore if the cat were a cartoon, his dumb tail would be shaped like a heart. Noir gave a long *meow*, licking his paw. The cat paused as he realized the staff girl wasn't watching him.

Noir turned back to Lucas, as if to say, *Why isn't it working?*

Lucas rolled his eyes at his friend. Noir had played this part in their schemes many times before. He was always the distraction, being that the city girls preferred a soft cat to pet over a smelly teenage boy. He wasn't used to being unacknowledged.

Lucas gave Noir as little attention as possible as the cat continued a doomed attempt to win the heart of the foreign staff wielder.

Purring, Noir weaved in between the girl's legs.

Seafrost jolted away from the feline, unfamiliar with Noir's way of flirting. The cat still persisted, placing his paw on her foot and mewing in a way that Lucas would never admit was adorable.

"What is it doing?" she demanded, knuckles white.

Noir purred louder.

"Lucas." She butchered the pronunciation of his name so severely that it grew near to the word "locust." And she sounded almost... afraid? "Lucas, what is it doing?"

"Stabbing me in the back," Lucas muttered. He picked up an old can and tossed it at Noir, who jumped and screeched and retreated. Pride bubbled up inside him. He had saved the stone-cold staff girl from a devious stray.

"But he has no blade." Seafrost stared after the cat, questions in her voice. When she glanced back at Lucas, he was chuckling.

"Well, it's not as cool as your 'blades,' but I have one. Wanna see?"

Seafrost nodded. For once, something besides getting home to Wonderland seemed to interest her. And her eyes were pretty. So clear and blue. Like the sky—*what?*

Lucas dug through his pockets, producing something his dad had given him a long time ago. A Swiss Army knife. He dangled it from his finger, held up by a key chain.

"That is no blade," Seafrost grumbled, losing all interest.

"Wait, wait, wait." Lucas caught the Swiss Army knife and turned it over in his palm. He held it out for her to see as he unfolded the tiny knife.

"Not all blades look the same," he said, smiling as she leaned forward with an awestruck expression. "This old thing, it can do everything. Look, there's even a corkscrew."

"Corkscrew?" Her pronunciation of that word also sounded off. Borderline British. Lucas could tell she wanted to touch it, so he handed it to her.

Seafrost marveled at the knife, pulling all the tools out at once. And Lucas leaned back, arms crossed, marveling at her. Her tanned skin, her strong build, her white-and-blue hair. He wondered what it looked like when it wasn't tied back in a braid.

He sat up, catching himself. *White hair? C'mon, who has white hair?*

Seafrost was twisting his Swiss Army knife into the wooden crate underneath her. He cringed.

"I give you my knife and you vandalize my furniture? I told you this is a rental. My landlord will be in contact."

She looked up, pausing her project. And though it was unlikely that she understood his joke at all, she smiled.

Lucas's cheeks inflamed. He ran a hand down his face, searching for the sentence he had prepared but finding nothing but the fact that he was screwed. Oh so screwed.

Noir hopped down from above, landing on his head. However clawful, Lucas was thankful for his friend's intervention.

"See?" he said, tossing an attention-deprived Noir aside. "I can share my blade."

And just like that, her smile vanished. Lucas heaved a sigh of relief. That smile was dangerous.

After having embedded the Swiss Army knife in the crate, Seafrost seemed lost on what else to do. Lucas cleared his throat, and she looked over at him.

"Speaking of sharing," he started, pushing himself to his feet. Seafrost mimicked him. "No, sit back down."

She obeyed.

"Are you hungry?"

She nodded eagerly.

"All right Frosty, close your eyes." At this, her brows furrowed. She gripped the staff with both hands.

"Oh come on." Lucas threw his hands up in a gesture of innocence.

She didn't even blink.

"You can trust me!" he said, even though he didn't even

trust himself. From atop a wall, Noir let out a hiss, calling the boy's bluff. Lucas shot the darned cat a warning glare.

Seafrost narrowed her eyes.

"I won't even touch you, I promise. You can turn around, if that's any better." And though Lucas's promises were worth less than the socks on his feet, Seafrost turned around slowly and waited.

"That's it." He laughed, getting right to work. He pulled his crate out from the wall and kicked cobwebs away. He shook out his only blanket and spread it out over the crate like a tablecloth.

"Make sure you dress up, Frosty. I'm taking you to the fanciest restaurant in New York City." He coughed. His blanket was a little dusty.

"I *am* dressed," she said. Her voice was getting warmer, nicer. And she was twisting his knife into a new hole in the crate.

Fishing through his collection of stolen goods, Lucas pulled out a flashlight and a strip of cloth. He turned on the flashlight, which was nearly out of battery. Perfect. He stood the flashlight up on his table crate and draped the cloth over it so that if you squinted and tilted your head, it might slightly resemble a candle.

Next, he rummaged through his clothes. Finding the cleanest shirt he owned and double-checking that her back was turned, he changed it. And then he spotted a tie he had taken right off the neck of a sleeping drunk. *Perfect.*

Lucas ran his hands through his hair and then turned

to Noir, who had found his way back to the boy. "How do I look?"

Noir propped his front paws on the boy's shoulders; a thorough examination. He tilted his little black head.

"That bad?" Lucas whispered.

Noir gave a firm lick to the boy's forehead, making his hair stand up. And then he was careening down the alley before Lucas could scold him.

The boy sighed but moved on quickly. Checking first to make sure the cat was out of sight, Lucas pried open his secret crate. Inside was his *good* stash. His most prized possession: candy bars in a jar.

He placed the jar on the table and seated himself on his knees. Lastly, Lucas did a breath check. He shuddered. And then he shrugged. "Okay, you can turn around now!"

Seafrost stood up. Her long braid whipped as she twisted around to face him. She stared at the candlelit dinner he had prepared.

He quickly got to his feet, having barely remembered to be chivalrous. He approached her and offered his arm.

She only watched him, expression extremely hard for him to decode.

"What? Is it the tie? I knew the tie was a dumb idea," he grumbled, nearly strangling himself trying to take the thing off. He froze as she took the tie into her own hands, tucking it under the collar of his shirt. He was scared to even move, for fear she would realize she had willingly touched him and change her mind.

Seafrost brushed off his shoulder. "This is the fanciest restaurant in New York City?" she asked, finally meeting his gaze. Up close, her eyes were even clearer. *Beautiful.*

For a moment, Lucas forgot he could speak.

"W-Well, the second fanciest," he stammered. He pretended to open a door and guide them inside. He pulled out Seafrost's imaginary chair for her.

"My lady," he said as she was seated. He rushed around the crate and sat across from her. "So," he said, sweeping the candy jar off the table so nothing obstructed his view. "Tell me about Wonder—I mean Beyond."

"It's in the sky," she said, pointing up. The first stars had made themselves known in the colorful sky. "I fight for my people."

"Uh-huh." Lucas nodded along.

"We don't have fancy restaurants like *this*," she said. Uh-oh. There was that smile again.

"Well, to be honest with you…" Lucas couldn't believe his own ears. But he kept speaking. "New York has much more to offer than this. There are far fancier restaurants, gardens… basically everywhere is better than here."

Seafrost leaned her face on her hand. "Back home, I like to walk in the garden. It's prettiest in the evening," she said.

Lucas reached into the candy jar and pulled out a chocolate bar. "In between kicking butts?" he asked, opening the bar and breaking it in half. He handed her the bigger half. Why did he hand her the bigger half? He'd never done that before.

Seafrost smiled again, but this time, her smile was sad. "I walk in the garden a lot, but I can't walk alone anymore. I have to stroll the gardens every morning with my betrothed."

Lucas froze, halfway through a big bite of chocolate.

"He's a... What is the word... Oh. Jerk." She sniffed the chocolate, completely unaware of Lucas's inner turmoil.

"Let me guess," he said, "the betrothal thing wasn't your call?"

She shook her head, nibbling on her bar. And then her eyes got wide. "What is this?" she cried.

"You don't have chocolate up there?" Lucas gasped. "May I speak to who's in charge?"

"That would be my uncle." Seafrost sighed.

"Also a jerk?"

Seafrost didn't answer him. She seemed to drift off into thought. Behind her, the staff lay unguarded. And for the first time since Seafrost sprang out of the staff, Lucas didn't even think about how he could take it.

"Wanna go to—"

Lucas was interrupted by a loud screech sounding down the alley. It was Noir. The cat dashed down the alley and then onto Lucas in a flurry of claws and spiky fur.

"Seriously?" the boy scowled, prying his unlucky cat off of him. Noir had the worst timing. But the thunder of footprints shifted the blame off of the cat and onto an approaching crowd.

Mr. Gredihans and a dozen or so men broke into view, charging down the alleyway. Lucas glanced from side to side, unfortunately coming to the conclusion that he had feared.

They were trapped.

The enemy was charging down the only way out. He shouldn't have been so stupid. What if they took the girl?

"Who are they?" Seafrost asked quietly, getting to her feet.

Lucas wasn't sure how to answer her. He didn't really feel like admitting that her staff had first belonged to the rich man before it fell into his possession. He also didn't feel like explaining that he was actually just a dirty thief, who had stolen the staff to secure his next meal. He started to pace.

"Lucas?" *Locust.*

"I'm not a swarming grasshopper!" he cried, hands in his hair.

"*What?*" Seafrost was now very, very confused.

The men filled the alley like *they* were locusts, swarming around the boy and the girl and the cat. Well, the boy and the girl. Noir had jumped ship.

Gredihans spied his expensive weapon leaning against the crate. "There it is," he growled. "That's my staff."

"This staff does not belong to you," Seafrost said

sharply. Her anger made Lucas consider jumping ship along with Noir.

"It's *mine*," Gredihan said.

"No." She stretched out her hand. The staff went soaring into her grasp. "It belongs to me."

Gredihans's jaw dropped. But he pointed a gnarly finger and managed to claim the staff was his one more time.

"Would anyone believe me if I said it was mine?" Lucas put into the argument, which was starting to sound a lot like the Five-year-old's who ended up ripping their doll in half. Lucas didn't want the staff to get broken. *He* was already broke enough.

Both Gredihans and Seafrost glared at him.

"No? Okay, okay. Just asking." Lucas was starting to get nervous.

Seafrost stepped towards the men.

Great. She's challenging them to a fight.

"Frosty, can you count?" Lucas hissed in a whisper. "Do they have math in your world? We're outnumbered. Severely. Maybe we should think about handing the staff over."

Seafrost didn't look at him. She stepped forward again, muscles rippling as she split her staff into the two blades. "A warrior does not surrender," she said, chin up, voice firm.

"But smart people do." Lucas grabbed her arm, fully intent on making a run for it. They could just steal the staff back later. Right now, Lucas didn't care about having a week's worth of food every day. He just wanted her to not die.

Seafrost jerked away from him, eyes cold and mean. Like when she had first appeared. Like the last thirty minutes had never happened.

Lucas stepped back, feeling slightly betrayed. If he started running now, he could probably get away. Vault over the wall. Continue dumpster diving for the rest of his life. Have an unlucky cat as his partner.

"Get her!" Gredihans cried, and the men advanced on the girl with the staff.

Time seemed to slow. Lucas was frozen. Both the angel and the devil on his shoulders told him to run.

Lucas yanked his trusty Swiss Army knife out of the wooden crate and found himself beside Seafrost. Sure, he'd only just met her. And sure, she was insufferably stubborn. *And* sure, he'd probably steal her staff later. But he couldn't leave her to Gredihans and his men. *Where was the fun in that?*

"If you want her staff," he called out, waving the corkscrew at Gredihans. "You'll have to fight us both." He glanced at Seafrost, whose sturdy exterior softened a little.

His hero moment ended quickly. Gredihans and his men pulled out their guns, and his dad's Swiss Army knife started to feel a little small.

"You don't know what a gun is, do you?" he murmured.

"You mean the small dull things they are pointing at us? Nothing compared to my blades."

"Oh gods," Lucas swore. Well, if he was going to die, might as well die beside a pretty girl.

"Last chance," Gredihans said. "Hand it over."

Technically, that's just what Seafrost did. She threw one of the blades. It skewered two of the men like a shish kebob before they could even fire. They stood there, pinned together. And when the blade retreated back into the girl's grasp, they fell down dead.

Chaos erupted. Seafrost's blades went flying, and Lucas ducked, trying not to lose his head. One of the men was on the ground beside him. He pointed his gun at Lucas.

Without even thinking, the boy drove the corkscrew into the man's hand. The man cried out in pain while Lucas grabbed his gun. "Thank you," he said, "and I'll take my knife back."

He rolled, prayed he could figure out how to not shoot himself, and then one by one, Lucas shot at the remaining men's ankles. With Seafrost's magic blades and Lucas's half decent aim, the pair was untouchable.

Gredihans's men began to flee. "What are you doing?" the rich bully yelled after them. "You're all cowards!"

Lucas started laughing, and then he realized as his pant leg was turning red that he had been shot. "We might wanna wrap this up, Frosty!" he said, a little hysterical. He had never been shot before. It wasn't very convenient.

Seafrost had both of her blades now. She faced Gredihans, and she threw them one after the other. Lucas waited for the man's dying wail.

He heard a gunshot instead.

Seafrost's blades clattered to the ground. She staggered, hand on her side. Her eyes found Lucas's. For once, she looked less like a warrior and more like a lost little girl. Her blue eyes were so, so sad. And she collapsed.

With a big-bellied laugh, Gredihans picked up one of the blades.

Lucas's heartbeat went wild as he threw himself at Gredihans. They grappled against the alley wall. Enraged, Lucas was somehow equal in strength. And then with a kick to Gredihans's knee, Lucas wrenched the blade out of his grasp.

Gredihans faced him, back against the wall, raising his gun with trembling hands. "Give me my staff, you filthy streetrat!"

Lucas smiled.

And Noir attacked from above, scratching and clawing at the man's face. Gredihans screamed and dropped his gun. Lucas kicked it out of reach, and then the rich man went running.

"It's Mr. Filthy Streetrat to you!" Lucas shouted. And then he leaned against the wall, catching his breath. The blade in his hands dripped with blood. And the girl reflected in it looked so sad. So tired.

Seafrost!

Noir was already beside Seafrost when Lucas hurriedly hobbled over.

The girl watched him placidly, one hand over the bullet hole in her side, the other stroking Noir's dark fur. Lucas gritted his teeth as he scooped her into his arms. He sat her up against their dinner table crate.

"I'm so sorry," Lucas said. "It's my fault. I stole the staff. It's my fault they were after you." He ripped the cloth on the flashlight off and pressed it against her wound, hoping to slow the bleeding.

Seafrost adjusted his tie, tucking it under his collar once more. As she moved, Noir cuddled up beside her and began licking a minor cut on her arm like a worried mother.

"Guns are bad," she said finally.

Lucas needed to get her to a hospital. He needed help.

"Don't worry one bit, Frosty," said Lucas. "I'm going to get you all fixed up, and then I'm going to take you home."

"Home?" she whispered.

"Yeah, I heard there's a bus leaving the city headed straight for Beyond. If you manage to stop bleeding, I think we can still catch it." Lucas didn't know why he wasn't running. He didn't know why he didn't want to take the staff anymore. Both the blades were up for grabs.

But the thought of leaving her made him feel sick.

"When we get there, you're taking me to the garden," he said softly, "in the evening. When you like it best." He pulled off his tie and wrapped it around her waist, securing the cloth over her wound. "And Noir will beat up your betrothed for you."

Seafrost didn't seem to understand him anymore. Her blue eyes were glassed over.

He moved to pick her up so he could make it to the main street. And then he could get her help. Everything would be okay if he could just get her to a doctor.

"Lucas," she whispered.

He stopped. She had said his name right.

She lifted a hand weakly. The blades floated over. With all of her strength, Seafrost drove the blades together and reassembled the staff. She reached for Lucas's hand.

"I trust you," she told him. And she gave him the staff, squeezing his palms over the cold metal.

"Seafrost?"

"It's yours."

——

"Looks like someone is ready for bed," CeCe said, jerking her thumb in Julian's direction. The boy's eyelids had gone from wide to droopy to shut, and now his breathing came evenly and his mouth was slightly ajar. Harmony wondered how the boy could possibly sleep at such an intense moment in the story. But then again, she wondered many things about Julian.

"Bedtime," Gramps chimed, rising off of the couch.

"No!" Harmony blurted before she could contain her frustration. "You can't just stop there!"

Gramps smiled at her. "I'll finish it tomorrow. Besides, we have to stretch out my stories if they're going to last six weeks. I don't have forty-two gut-wrenching tales—that I can remember correctly, at least."

CeCe tried to wake Julian, but when that didn't work, she scooped him up and carried him to his room.

"Off to bed, sweetie," Gramps said, patting Harmony on the shoulder.

"You sure you don't want to tell me the ending?"

"I'm super sure." He chuckled.

Harmony sighed, wanting nothing more than to know how his story ended. But then she hugged her grandfather tightly and then ran up the stairs, escaping to her bedroom.

It had been a long time since Harmony had been passionate about anything, but that night, she couldn't stop thinking about the boy and his cat and the girl with a staff. She spent hours sketching out how they appeared in her head. Lucas, tall and lanky and wearing a smirk; Noir with big eyes and bread in his mouth; Seafrost with her long braid and intricate staff.

And when her wrist was tired, Harmony lay awake in bed, unable to close her eyes. She longed to hear more, to find out if Seafrost lived and if she ever got to go home. Harmony knew what it felt like to be thrown into a whole new world.

She rolled over. Her clock read 3:17 a.m.

Harmony rose out of the comfort of her bed and wandered downstairs. The house was silent as she made her way into the library, thinking that a good book might settle her thoughts and make her sleepy. She scanned through the book titles, her eyes resting on one named: *All You Need to Know about Cats*. It wasn't her ideal book, but she didn't really like reading anyway. She shrugged and pulled it out, immediately dropping the book with a gasp of surprise.

That's when the book shelf moved. It slid to the side without sound, revealing a dimly illuminated staircase. Without stopping to go over the reasons on why she shouldn't descend it, Harmony did just that.

She counted twenty-three steps that led into a rectangular room. Inside were lots of strange artifacts, consisting of a sword embroidered with diamonds, a carved wooden goose with rubies as eyes, and what looked like the head of a cow, perfectly preserved. But the item that caught Harmony's attention was on display, standing in a glass case.

A staff.

Her thoughts went immediately to Seafrost. The staff seemed to fit Gramps's description exactly. It even looked like her own drawing of it.

Could it be? She stepped closer to the case. *No, it couldn't.* Surely she was dreaming. But as Harmony reached out to touch the glass, the staff shattered through the display case and flew right into her outstretched hand.

And just like that, Harmony felt the overwhelming realization dawn upon her that the impossible was not unusual here in her grandparents' house.

This was going to be an interesting summer.

Ellipsis

The day I rode without training wheels was the first time I remember you telling me you loved me. That day, the Irvine sun pierced down our backs and tears fell from your pores. You were singing along to "Let It Be," which hummed from your favorite speaker.

"Time to take off the training wheels, son." Each word came with spit, dribbling down your chin. "See what you're made of." Bones and skin and mostly water and some other fluids and a little bit of you.

You, on your knees, wrenched off the wheels and laid them in the trunk, beneath a lint-covered blanket and candy wrappers and boxes of tissues I'd need later. I sat on the triangular seat, paralyzed. You buckled my helmet so tight that when I swallowed, it seemed close to snapping. My hands wrapped, trembling, around the handles.

"I'm right here," you said. "I won't let you fall."

I—eight years old—believed you, and imagined you

turned the ground into a trampoline for me. I believed you, because you could do anything. You could turn me insusceptible to pain; you would never inflict it. I believed you, and I ended up with three bleeding scars like dots in a row on my kneecap: a distorted ellipsis.

— — — — —

You wouldn't just let me fall. You'd be the one to push me to the ground—proverbially, sometimes literally. And now I have to stand up here and talk about how I miss you, how I wish we could've had five more minutes, how there were so many things I wish I could've told you.

It's a small service, and everyone here is selfishly weeping, muffled, into handkerchiefs. I hope you are okay, but not happy. I hope you are safe, but not at peace. I hope you are part of our favorite constellation—the one you used to show me, Sagittarius, *archer*—but not blinking down at me, aiming your arrow and preparing to shoot.

The ellipsis faded some twenty years ago, before I left for college, but there are others still there, constellations you left me with, so deep under my skin that for a long time during the surrogate's pregnancy, I wondered if my daughter would be born with indentations.

— — — — —

We were at the same abandoned parking lot, but this time there were different pedals at my feet. Brake and accelerate. You were sitting shotgun, and you loved to tell me the name's origin: back then, the shotgun-armed guard would sit there. ("Back when?" I'd ask. "Just... then.")

Your hat covered your raven hair and cast a shadow upon your eyes, and I wondered if you could see me. "How's that girl? The pretty one we ran into at Earl's Groceries the other day?"

"Oh, you mean Calliope?"

"Yeah, her. You said she was in your math class?" You pursed your lips.

"Oh, yeah, Cal's good." I placed my water in the cupholder. "I think she's been working on some history research thing. Why?"

"No, just... girls like boyfriends who can drive."

I managed a stilted chuckle, realizing you didn't know me at all, realizing you probably never would. I grasped the wheel and pressed my right foot on the acceleration pedal. You mimed what to do with an invisible wheel in your hands.

"Good, good... you're doing a good job." Just good. Your affirmations continued for a little while, but great, amazing, super—they weren't in your vocabulary. You weren't looking at me. It was as if you were waiting for me to mess up, as if you wanted me to. "Good, good—stop!" There was another car, silver and gleaming from the sun. Your voice was like a metal spoon falling onto the floor, ringing, clashing, echoing. *Stop!*

I slammed my foot on the brake and together we lurched forward. Your forehead hit against the metal and began to bleed a bit from the top. Thin red tears slid down. Your face remained a statue—every curve and wrinkle frozen—as you dabbed a tissue on the blood.

"I'm sorry," I whispered. "Dad, I'm sorry. Are you okay?"

You were silent, shooting at me with your shotgun and a lethal glare.

My lips began to quiver. "Do you want to take over? Dad? Are you—"

"Accelerate." You folded the tissue so the blood was hidden and tucked it into the pocket of your jeans. You had already stopped bleeding, and there was nothing left but a faint dab of redness. "Go. Accelerate."

I nodded, tears blurring my vision. Beyond the window, the sky was veiled in a slight haze. The tears kept coming. The world became blurrier and blurrier before me.

"Drive." Your voice was like lightning and you were Zeus. Spit bubbled on your bottom lip. "Drive!"

I let my head fall against the leathery wheel, crying, sighing, wishing that another car would come and crash into us, and I'd get hurt or worse, and then finally you could tell me it would all be okay even if it wouldn't be, and you would be my dad, and maybe you would finally feel something for me.

All I could see was blackness as I shut my eyes against the wheel. Then your hands clawed into my hair, jerked my head upward. "Fucking sissy. Stop crying." Your palm was ice against my cheek. The first time you hit me was almost like an accident. "You'll never be able to drive."

———————

I can still feel the red mark you left, like phantom pain, stinging extra today. I smile at Sabrina in the rearview mirror. Her black funeral dress doesn't even look sad on her. She is so good and precious, with hair a majestic auburn that bears no resemblance to yours. Each of her 318 freckles (we counted once) composes my heart.

"Are you okay, Daddy?"

I nod, staring ahead at the same sky you and I used to drive under, over the same bumpy road. You would blame the bumps on me.

"Where is Grandpa now?" Sabrina asks. "What happens when you die?"

Javier places a gentle hand on my shoulder. "Sab, honey, let's not—"

"That's all right. I wonder the same thing a lot," I say. There is a red light. "Like, yes, part of me thinks that you suddenly stop existing, and everything turns to black, and the world goes on without you. But if so many people believe in heaven and hell and all that, there's gotta be some truth to it, you know?"

"So then where is Grandpa? Heaven or hell?" She asks the same way she asks whether seven times eight is fifty-six or fifty-eight, or whether my favorite color is orange or blue. *Heaven or hell?*

"Sab!" Javier shuts her down, but her words conjure up an image of you: your left half charred and red, your right half aglow.

Aglow, like when you pretended to be a sports announcer and made me feel important; charred and red, because I never really liked sports. In flames, because all of your love for me was contained in a hard yellow lacrosse ball, and I was crappy at cradling it close, and even worse at scooping it off the ground, and when you threw it at me, I seldom caught it. I let it fall away. I raced after it and watched it roll farther and farther the more I tried to scoop it up. You said, "Two hands, two hands," but I was so sick and tired. You didn't deserve both of my hands anymore.

When I was a teenager, I'd check my watch frantically as the sun began to set, wishing the time would pass slower and dreading your stomps through the doorway. You brought the smell of rubble and dirt into our household each night. We were just afloat. I imagined the mystery of your day-to-day, imagined you standing with a crowd of guys, smoking cigarettes and complaining about your wives. It didn't occur to me until I was well into my twenties that maybe your dad did the same, and maybe you're not the one to blame.

Javier and I met in college and fell in love quickly. You referred to him as my "friend," if you referred to him at all. You left for the bathroom halfway through our wedding ceremony and didn't return until the reception. Did you think I wouldn't notice the empty white chair where my father should have been? Did you think I didn't see the way Mom grabbed your forearm, but you wriggled from her grip and sidled conspicuously up the aisle?

You died in a plane accident. Your death came out of nowhere, which is easier than fading away from disease, slowly descending. You always wanted me to fly, and you died doing it.

— — — — — —

Your funeral was a couple of weeks ago, and I should be sadder than I am. Most of the time, I'm simply numb. Sometimes, when I pull up the picture on my phone—the one Mom took of us at high school graduation—I recall the moment so vividly that my head itches from the graduation cap. I feel your hands around my shoulders. And then I think about the other things those hands did, the bad things.

"Whatcha lookin' at?" Sab appears at the entryway, holding her blue blankie. Her ponytail hangs messily by the side of her neck.

"Just some work emails." I close out the picture. "You should be sleeping, Sab. You've got school tomorrow." Through the window, the sky is speckled with faint constellations.

"I know. But everytime I close my eyes, I start having this weird dream." She lies beside me on the couch. "There are snakes all over the ground, biting at my feet."

"Well, that can't be good." I pull her into an embrace. "Sleep right here. Maybe if we put our heads together, we'll have the same dream."

She giggles. "I don't know if that's how it works, Daddy. Besides, I'm not really tired."

"I am."

"Can I crack your knuckles?"

"No," I grumble.

Sabrina wraps her tiny fingers around my index finger and pushes it all the way in until the bone cracks.

"Ouch. Don't do that, Sab."

She laughs, doing the same with my middle finger.

"Sabrina, please stop."

Her unruly laughter pierces through my ears. She takes my pinky finger. My pain is somehow so funny to her. *Ouch.* It's a reflex; I don't mean to do it. I jerk my hand out of her grip, and my pinky nail knocks against her lip. My hand begins to shake. Blood trickles from a cut, a line on her top lip. It's just a little blood, just a small bit.

Her nostrils twitch. I did this. I stare into my palm and see the same wrinkles you had.

Her cries grow, music faded into discord. The blood is gone—she's licked it off—but it's there, bright, everywhere, all over her and me.

She stares at me as if I'm the monster under her bed. I'm one of the snakes pecking at her feet.

"I'm so sorry, Sab. I'm so—let me get paper towels." I am immobile.

Her chest rises and falls quickly. She's scared of me. Sab backs away from the bed, running for Javier. "Daddy, Daddy."

– — — — — —

Your favorite flowers were dandelions. You always told me it was because they were actually weeds, and you liked that not everyone knew that. Weeds could be beautiful. I plucked all the dandelions I could find this morning and tied them with a satin ribbon. So here are some dandelions. I hope they find you well.

Martin H. Sullivan

6 October 1956

12 June 2021

Father, Son, Husband

Reading your tombstone, it feels as if the breeze that erects the hairs on my forearms is you, blowing air at me, begging to be noticed above the many with which you share the sky. I can hear you singing Beatles songs, cradling me in your arms—arms that warmed me when I shivered; arms that held me in the air when you sang, "Zoom zoom zoom, we're going to the moon;" arms that "knocked some sense into me;" arms that my own were beginning to replicate last night; arms that my own can never replicate again; arms that didn't save me when I fell off my bike, when three round scars appeared on my kneecap, like an ellipsis.

The End of Us

Hasfariza Hassan, Malaysia

@hxtiku:
"Time is golden," they used to whisper,
You forgot,
They forgot,
Why do I still remember?
Stuck and stagnant,
Still as water,
I wonder why I'm still indulging in this,
My feet frozen,
Immovable,
As silent conversations overtake me,
This chapter has ended,
I know it well,
Unfair that I'm still here,
Why do I remember the forgotten so clearly?
Even the minuscule details,
"A curse, it is,"

My eyes begin to betray me,
The emotions slowly seep out.

@yxnke:
The melancholy fills my heart.
The truth unveils.
You have long forgotten me,
Faded into an old photograph,
That's all I had become.
I used to be your person,
To whom you recounted your clumsy acts.
The weird questions you would ponder over,
Only your beautifully-wired mind could think of,
The eccentric wit that embodied you,
The urges that you had to blurt out,
Unable to contain your excitement,
And the thoughts that infiltrate your mind;
Only I could tell.

@hxtiku:
Why does my heart ache?
Why did you not warn me sooner?
Perhaps you did whilst I turned a blind eye.
I took that form of silence as a sign of hope.
How wrong I was.
Unfortunately, the memories remain.

My mind plays them like a movie.
Moment after moment,
Time,
After time,
Wistfulness fills my soul.
Just as I think I'm moving on.
Your presence startles me once more.

@yxnke:
Perhaps you're angry and you think I never cared.
My memories say otherwise,
Primary school to high school,
You and I were like Milo trucks and sports day:
Necessary together.
You in your baju kurung and me in my prefect uniform,
Perhaps that was the first sign,
Our friendship was temporary,
Always meant for just this chapter.

@hxtiku:
Eleven years down the drain.
Nostalgia creeps up on me,
The connection between us withered.
I likened us to a sturdy oak tree,
Yet we turned out to be hollow,
The deep roots beneath the ground meaningless,

I wonder if I could take it all back.
What if I never sat beside you in standard one?[1]
Maybe your disappearance wouldn't have affected me as much,
The maybes and buts can't turn back time,
The photographs in my mind will forever remain,
But for you, they have long ceased.

@yxnke:
"Saya tak akan lepaskan awak,"[2]
I used to say.
Truth be told,
You knew this day would come.
I never meant for it to be a lie,
As always I wish you the best.
All I ever wanted,
Was for you to be happy and healthy.
I pray that you forget me.
Forgive me for not letting our friendship be.

@hxtiku:
My heart burns,
Fiery blaze consuming it all.
Ashes only remain,
After the pain and suffering, shall I see a glimpse of hope?

Meeting you wasn't a tragedy,
Even though it ended tragically,
It was an adventure I shall never forget.
Losing you was like losing a limb,
My anguish of losing you may heal,
The cracks in the broken glass are still present,
I realized that you weren't meant for every chapter of my
life.
I wish the red strings that connected us had not snapped,
But most of all, I thank and cherish our time together.

@hxtiku:
Was it really a curse, after all?
"No, a blessing," the voice murmured,
For the first time,
I felt it, too.
No longer in the murky waters,
My eyes filled with glee.

1. Standard one is first grade or year one.
2. "I won't let you go."

Last

Molly Hamilton, Ohio

last
\ 'last \

1. Coming after all the others; final in order, sequence, or time:

> This moment was the *last* of everything. *Last* kiss, *last* touch, *last* word, *last* look. But not the *last* time she'd cross his mind. Not the *last* time she'd nearly drown herself over him.

2. At the time next preceding the present:

> *Last* year, they gripped each other's hands like that was the only thing that could keep the madness from sinking in through their palms. *Last* spring, her mother died. *Last* June, his father was arrested for murder. *Last* night, they whispered promises in the space between thin sheets and broke every one in the light of morning.

3. Final:

> In their *last* moments together, words tangled and
> stuck to his tongue, echoed in his head until he
> thought it might explode. He didn't speak, but his
> *last* thought was that he should have.

4. Ultimate or conclusive:

> He let her have the *last* word. She
> was a storm, and he was weak to
> her. She said go; he went.

5. Being the only one remaining:

> He used up his *last* bit of strength to
> walk away from her. She cried away
> every *last* drop of courage.

6. Most recent:

> She was *last* seen wearing his brown sweater.

7. Least probable, suitable, or desirable:

> Sleep was the *last* thing he should do, but
> failure weighed his eyelids down, so he did.

8. The final appearance, experience, or mention:

> She was gone. That was the *last* anyone would
> say of it. Her friends, his friends, no one cared.

9. To remain in existence:

> He couldn't make a relationship *last* after her.
> No one fit the mold he'd cast. No one could fix
> the broken part of him.

10. At length, finally:

> At *last*, he got tired of the hole
> shaped like her in his life.

11. To endure:

> He didn't know if his will to go on
> without her would *last*.

THE AUTHORS

Danielle N. Bartholet is an aspiring author of YA historical fiction, with her debut novel *On an Island of Broken Hope* releasing Fall 2023. She also hopes to release a poetry collection in 2022. She lives in Texas and enjoys reading, crocheting, and dark academia clothing. Instagram/TikTok: danibwriting. Podcast: *The Write Path with Dani B.*

Isabella Fauber is a sixteen-year-old from New York. She loves spending time outdoors with her dog, playing soccer, sketching fashion designs, and enjoying time with friends and family. Isabella is deeply passionate about autoimmune research and published an article with the Hospital for Special Surgery on antiphospholipid syndrome and the gut microbiome. "Ethereal Scar" is her first publication of poetry.

Heather Kirchhoff lives in Missouri with her husband, dog, two cats, and several fish. She became a bookworm back in sixth grade when her teacher suggested the Phantom Stallion series by Terri Farley and instantly fell in love. When Heather isn't writing, she enjoys reading, taking pictures, going on walks, and spending time with family and friends. Richelle Mead, Alyson Noel, and Stephenie Meyer inspired her to write when she was thirteen.

María F. Bergero was born and raised in Argentina, but now finds herself traveling around the world. She has mostly written fantasy and sci-fi short stories and has just finished her first full-length novel. In her stories, you can find afterlives, magical teas, ghostly animals, and romance, but the main element that's present in all of her pieces is the complexity of human nature. No matter where, you'll find her reading, writing, or drinking tea—regular, non-magical tea, of course.

Maja Zajaczkowska was born 29th of May in the year 2000 in the twin city Zgorzelec-Görlitz. She is a Polish writer, painter, and literature student based in Poland and Germany. Her work ranges from avant-garde postmodern poetry to experimental fiction. Maja's art is inspired by bohemian art movements, the post-Soviet world, and it also explores the depths of human consciousness. Instagram: @ insolentsorrow.

Molly Hamilton lives in Ohio with her partner and two cats. Her interests include myths, sagas, and anything Viking related. She writes poetry, fantasy novels, and the occasional D&D campaign. When she isn't writing or at her job as a cake decorator, Molly is most often sewing or working on her planner.

Lauren Redwood is a young adult writer, short story-teller, and poet. She is the author of two poems, "Under the Shadow of the Tent" and "Cold Days" published by Gary Barwin. She attends Sheridan College for a bachelor's in creative writing & publishing.

An avid reader who has a vivid imagination, **Hasfariza Hassan** is a writer who resides in the busy city of Selangor in Malaysia. She is an eighteen-year-old currently studying A-levels at Sunway College. She has a fascination with questions and likes to analyze things from different perspectives. Hasfariza loves exploring other cultures and languages, especially since she grew up in Malaysia and Indiana, USA. Her overactive imagination inspired her to write at the age of four, delving her into the world of fantasy, and she hopes to use her writing as a platform to give a voice to those who are unrepresented. Instagram: @Hasfariza_hassan.

Sophia Lind is a sixteen-year-old junior in high school from Westchester, New York. When Sophia isn't writing, she is feeding her creativity through traveling around New York City, watching sunsets, or sitting on her patio reading a book. She's inspired by the people she meets and her elaborate dreams.

Sowon Kim, born in South Korea, is an author, translator, and social entrepreneur. As the daughter of missionaries, she moved to Peru with her family when she was just three months old. Sowon translated *Leaving Wishville* from English to Spanish when she was fourteen years old and published *A Gleaming Shard of Glass*, her debut novel, at the age of fifteen.

Alexandria Johnson is an emerging fantasy writer and poet based in Malaysia. Her poetry has appeared in *The Star* local newspaper in conjunction with International Women's Day, *iRiS Magazine* #1, *The Poet's Haven Digest* #4, *Spillwords Press, Noctivagant Press*, and she has also won a consolation prize in the ASiS Poetry Competition. She can be found on Instagram @alexwritesandsings.

Sophie Miller is a high school senior from Westchester, New York. She is an aspiring novelist and edits the *Parent Coach* blog, striving to use her writing to fight psychological stigma. Sophie is a Stephen King superfan, a Harry Potter fanatic, and enjoys playing soccer and the piano in her spare time.

MC Pending is a teenage author who published her debut novel, *Untouchable*, in the summer of 2021. She is currently writing the sequel while being a sophomore at her university. She has loved expanding her platform and connecting with readers on Instagram throughout her publishing process.

Alex Cheng is a seventeen-year-old writer who specializes in short stories and poetry, and is currently working on his first novel. His work has been recognized by Scholastic Art & Writing Awards. Alex is from Ridgefield, Connecticut, and when he is not writing, he is spending time with family and friends, playing soccer and basketball, or reading. Find Alex on Instagram @alex.cheng2.

Alexandra Elwell was born and raised in Manhattan, fostering her love of writing and art. She is currently a high school junior and has been published in the *Potted Purple* magazine and *The Vision* magazine. Her creative passions have always been evident, manifesting in paintings, creative writing pieces, and essays. To her, the words she dusts onto the blank pages under her pen provide her with a special kind of solace and therapeutic moments.

Kimberly Swartz was born in California and moved to Washington State when she was three. Since then, she has spent most of her childhood exploring and traveling before becoming interested in writing at age eleven. Now, she is working on her associate's degree at Lower Columbia College as she works on her first novel.

THE EDITOR

Hudson Warm is a junior in high school in New York. She is the author of two young adult novels: *Academy for the Gifted,* a new thriller, won a Scholastic Gold Key and an Indie Excellence Award for Young Adult Fiction. *Not the Heir,* a fantasy, won a First Place Youth Author Fiction Purple Dragonfly Award and was featured on Katie Couric's "Books for Young Readers." Her short stories, flash fiction, and poetry have been recognized by the Scholastic Art & Writing Awards, won first prize for fiction in the 2021 Chappaqua Library Young Writers Contest, and have appeared in several publications. In addition to writing stories, Hudson enjoys singing and songwriting. Her songs are available on most musical platforms. She is the editor in chief of her school literary magazine, *The Vision*, and a first reader for *Polyphony Lit*.

Find Hudson online

WWW.HUDSONWARM.COM

Instagram: @hudsonwarmbooks

ACKNOWLEDGEMENTS

This project truly was a collaborative process. Curating this collection was like putting puzzle pieces together, in an order that told a moving story. All of my heart went into crafting and editing this collection. But I really could not have done any of this without each and every one of these amazing voices, so thank you to all of the writers that chose to trust me with their stories and poetry.

This project allowed me to unite my passions for writing and editing. When I called for submissions, I had no idea what would happen. Seeing people repost and submit right away fueled me to keep going. Thank you to all of the people who supported me on this journey.

Greg and Natalia Leigh at Enchanted Ink Publishing: You made this process, as always, so fun and exciting. The formatting and blurb editing you do never fails to amaze me. Thank you also to Chelsea for proofreading. I appreciate your diligence more than you know.

Damonza Cover Design: Thank you for working with me through the seventeen drafts. You put up with my perfectionism with extreme professionalism and made prompt edits. I absolutely adore the final cover; it reflects the collection perfectly.

Mom—thank you for being my daily inspiration. You encouraged me and stood by me through the challenges of this project. Dad—thank you for helping me with the contracts and overall being the best dad ever. Sasha—your presence brings me so much joy. Thank you for being my sister by chance, best friend by choice.

Thank you to the people in my life that make me smile every day—Harry, Bella, Mason, Emily, Alex, Ava, and all of the rest. Thank you to all of my teachers at Hackley School and Writopia for always being so supportive.

And lastly, thank you *you* so much, truly, for reading this collection.